#1 RETURN TO FOREVERWARE

Avon Books are available at special quantity discounts for bulk
purchases for sales promotions, premiums, fund raising or educa-
tional use. Special books, or book excerpts, can also be created to
fit specific needs.

For details write or telephone the office of the Director of Special
Markets, Avon Books, Dept. FP, 1350 Avenue of the Americas,
New York, New York 10019, 1-800-238-0658.

#1 RETURN TO FOREVERWARE

MIKE FORD

AN AVON CAMELOT BOOK

AVON BOOKS
A division of
The Hearst Corporation
1350 Avenue of the Americas
New York, New York 10019

Copyright © 1997 by Hearst Entertainment, Inc.
Based on the Hearst Entertainment television series entitled "Eerie Indiana"
Excerpt from *Eerie Indiana #2: Bureau of Lost* copyright © 1997 by Hearst Entertainment, Inc.
Published by arrangement with Hearst Entertainment, Inc.
Visit our website at **http://AvonBooks.com**
Library of Congress Catalog Card Number: 97-93490
ISBN: 0-380-79774-7
RL: 4.6

First Avon Camelot Printing: October 1997

CAMELOT TRADEMARK REG. U.S. PAT. OFF. AND IN OTHER COUNTRIES, MARCA REGISTRADA, HECHO EN U.S.A.

Printed in the U.S.A.

OPM   10 9 8 7 6 5 4 3 2 1

PROLOGUE

PROLOGUE

My name is Marshall Teller. Not too long ago, I was living in New Jersey, just across the river from New York City. It was crowded, polluted, and full of crime. I loved it. But my parents wanted a better life for my sister and me. So we moved to a place so wholesome, so squeaky clean, so ordinary that you could only find it on TV: Eerie, Indiana.

It's the American Dream come true, right? Wrong. Sure, my new hometown *looks* normal enough. But look again. Underneath, it's crawling with strange stuff. Item: Elvis lives on my paper route. Item: Bigfoot eats out of my trash. Item: I see unexplained flashing lights in the sky at least once a week. No one believes me, but Eerie is the center of weirdness for the entire planet.

Since I moved here, I've been attacked by a werewolf, had my brain sucked out and put back in, delivered a letter for a ghost, and been stalked by a grudge-bearing tornado named Bob. Every time something strange happens, I think my life can't get any more peculiar. But then I turn a corner and there's something even stranger waiting for me. But no matter how weird Eerie gets, nobody else seems to notice.

Nobody except my friend Simon Holmes, that is. Simon's my next-door neighbor. He's lived in Eerie his whole life, and he's the only other person who knows just how freaky this place is. Together, we've been keeping a record of all the stuff that happens around here. We've faced some of Eerie's most bizarre inhabitants and lived to tell about it, from the talking dogs that tried to take over the city to the crazy gray-haired kid who lives in the old abandoned mill and can't remember who he is. I told you this place was weird.

Still don't believe me? You will.

1

*I*t all started Saturday morning at breakfast, when my father came in and sat down across the table from me. He was dressed for work. I remembered that he was going to be working overtime at the office for the next two months. He'd even have to work a few hours on the weekends.

"So, Marshall, what are you doing in your spare time these days?" he asked me.

I looked up from my bowl of cereal. Dad was staring at me expectantly over his cup of coffee, as though he were waiting for me to make some fantastic announcement about how I was designing a telecommunications satellite or working on a cure for the common cold or something. Instead, all I could say was, "Um, I don't really know. Hanging out, my paper route. You know, the normal stuff."

Dad smiled his I-have-a-great-idea smile, the one that always means he's about to say something I don't want to hear, like "Wouldn't this be a great day to mow the lawn?" or "Isn't it time to get that hair cut again?" He took a deep breath. Then he said the fateful words no kid *ever* wants to hear: "Maybe you should think about getting a weekend job. You might find it a lot more exciting than sitting around watching TV."

I groaned. It was as if he'd dumped a big bucket of ice-cold water all over my day. I guess he figured that since he was going to be working extra time, I should be too. That didn't seem at all fair to me, but Dad was on a roll.

"I always had jobs when I was your age," he said, as though he were remembering the best times of his life. "Did me a world of good. Got me ready for the real world."

What I wanted to say was, "Yeah, but the real world around here is full of aliens and werewolves and you don't even know it, so how much good did that summer job do you?" But what I said was, "Uh-huh."

I started to remind him about my morning paper route again but just then my older sister, Syndi, came into the kitchen. She opened the refrigerator and poured herself a glass of orange juice. Desperate for an escape, I tried to use her as a way out of my situation.

"Syndi doesn't do anything on weekends," I said hastily.

Syndi popped some slices of bread into the toaster. "Wrong again, wonder brain. I'm working with Mom down at the mall."

My mother runs a party-planning business at a shop downtown. I've never heard of anyone in Eerie ever having a party, but she seems to be doing okay. I think she caters a lot of funerals or something.

"Hey, here's a thought," my dad said. "How would you like to work with me at the office? They need people to assist with the special project I'm working on. It's a—you know—one of those, well . . ."

I should explain that my dad works for Things, Incorporated, Eerie's biggest company. They test products there before they go on the market in other cities. They figure if a product does well here, it will do well anywhere, since Eerie is, statistically speaking, the most normal place on the planet. I guess it depends on whose statistics you use. Or what planet.

Anyway, my dad is some kind of engineer at Things, Inc., but we aren't really sure what he does. Every night he comes home whistling and happy, and when Mom asks him how his day went, he always says, "Oh, just fine. Couldn't be better." But whenever I ask him what it is he's working on, he gets this funny look on his face and says, "You know, I can't seem to remember." I didn't know what they were doing to him over there, but I was pretty sure I didn't want to find out. I tried to think of a good excuse to get out of accepting his offer.

"I think maybe I'll just look around first and see what's out there," I said, hoping he'd buy it.

Dad smiled again. "Okay," he said. "Just let me know if you can't find anything else. I know they're looking for boys in the product-testing department. You'd be perfect for that."

I definitely didn't want to test *anything* made in Eerie. Who knew what it would do to me?

"Thanks, Dad," I said quickly. "But I'm pretty sure I'll be able to find something right away."

"Maybe you can get a job at the mall," said Syndi. "You could work at the movie theater. I hear they let the ticket-takers have free popcorn."

I pictured myself in the dorky uniform they made the employees wear at the theater, taking tickets all day from screaming kids who came to see the latest cartoon. I imagined the kids from school seeing me there. "No, thanks," I said. "I'd rather do something a little less damaging to my social life, such as it is."

"Whatever," said Syndi. "I know *I'd* be into free popcorn."

She took her toast and went back upstairs. Dad looked at his watch. "What time is it?" he asked.

"Almost eight-twenty," I said, checking the clock on the wall.

"Holy crow," Dad exclaimed. "I'm late. Darn watch stopped again. It's been giving me trouble ever since I started working on that new nuclear whatsamajiggy. You know, the thing that . . . Oh, well, I can't remember what it does. It dries hair, or sprays paint, or something. Anyway, I'd better go."

He left a minute later, taking the butter dish with him but leaving his briefcase on the stove. As he was heading out the door, Simon came walking in.

"Hey, Mars."

"Hey, Simon. What's on the agenda for this day of glorious freedom?"

Simon sighed. "My dad says I have to get a job," he said sadly. "He ran into your dad at the hardware store the other day and he suggested it."

"I apologize on behalf of my dad," I said. "So much for finding out what's *really* in the basement of the old Scudder mansion." For months, Simon and I had been planning an expedition into Eerie's most famous haunted house. Rumor was that no one who went in ever came out again. We suspected they were all still in there, but we needed proof. Now we would have to wait.

Simon unfolded the copy of the *Eerie Examiner* that my dad had left sitting on the table. "I guess we should look through the help wanted ads," he said.

The two of us turned to the back of the paper and

scanned through the list of available weekend jobs, looking for something that wouldn't be too horrible.

"Want to be a part-time grave digger?" Simon asked, pointing to an ad halfway down the page promising good pay and convenient hours.

"In the Eerie cemetery?" I said.

Simon shook his head. "You're right. Too risky. We need something nice and safe."

We kept going, ruling out being snake salesmen at Eerie Pets, trash sorters at the Eerie landfill, and assistant butchers at Eerie Meats. In fact, we had read almost all of the ads without finding anything that wasn't dangerous to our well-being. I was beginning to think that I'd have to take my dad's offer after all. Then Simon noticed something.

"Hey, look at this," he said. Tucked away in the corner of the last page was a small ad. It read:

BOY WANTED FOR ODD JOB.
AFTER SCHOOL, WEEKENDS.
GOOD BENEFITS. NO QUESTIONS ASKED.

"Odd job?" I said. "Shouldn't it be odd jobs?"

"It's probably just a printing mistake," said Simon, ripping the ad out and putting it in his pocket. "Come on. Let's go check it out."

"But they only want one kid," I said.

"We don't have any other leads," said Simon. "Besides, maybe whoever it is could use two people. It can't hurt to just go and see what it is."

That's where he was wrong.

2

We rode our bikes to the address listed in the ad. The house looked perfectly ordinary, just like all the other houses on the street. It was white with blue trim, and there was a window box filled with red geraniums at each window. There was a wood-paneled station wagon parked in the driveway, and the lawn was carefully mowed. There was even a white picket fence across the front, with roses climbing up it.

"I wonder what they need help with," I said. "This place looks absolutely spotless."

We parked our bikes by the fence and walked up to the front door. Simon rang the bell, and we waited. A minute later the door was opened by a woman wearing a lime green polyester pants suit and lots of blue eye shadow. Her dark hair was brushed back on either side of her head like a pair of wings. She looked just like my mother did in a picture I'd seen of her from her high school yearbook. Only that picture had been taken in the 1970s.

"Can I help you?" she said.

"We're here about the ad," Simon said. "You know, for the job. I'm Simon. This is my friend Marshall."

The woman looked at Simon, then at me. She seemed to be studying us carefully. Finally she smiled. "I'm Mrs. Stewart," she said. "Why don't you come in?"

We went inside. Mrs. Stewart looked around outside, as though checking to see if anyone else was out there, then shut the door. She led us into her living room, which was covered in gold carpeting. "Have a seat," she said, pointing to the orange and green striped sofa. "I'll just go get us all something to drink."

We sat down while she disappeared into the kitchen.

"There's something weird about this place," I whispered to Simon. "It looks like it hasn't been redecorated since the 1970s. Look at all the macramé plant holders. And those paintings of the kids with the big eyes holding daisies. They're creepy."

"I don't know," Simon said. "I kind of like it. It's cool. Very retro."

Mrs. Stewart came back in with a tray, which she set down on the glass-topped coffee table. "Here," she said, handing us each a glass of purple liquid. "I hope you like grape Nehi."

"Nehi!" said Simon. "Wow! I haven't had this since we visited my grandmother and she had a case of it in the basement. This stuff is great. I didn't think they made it anymore.''

Mrs. Stewart beamed at him. ''I'm so glad you like it,'' she said. ''I have so much of it left over from . . . from before.'' She picked up a plate and offered it to us. ''Would you care for a pig in a blanket?''

I looked at the things on the plate. They looked like miniature hot dogs rolled up in dough. They had been toasted, and there was a toothpick stuck through each one. To tell the truth, they looked pretty weird. But I didn't want to offend her, so I picked one up and took a bite. To my surprise, it was actually pretty good.

''This is really amazing,'' I said with my mouth full. ''I've never had one before.''

She smiled. ''Thank you so much. I made them myself. I got the recipe out of one of my magazines.'' She picked up an issue of *Perfect Homemaker* magazine and showed it to me. The date on the cover was July 1976. In fact, all of the magazines on the table were from 1976. One showed a picture of a man with big teeth grinning from ear to ear. PRESIDENT CARTER? said the headline.

Mrs. Stewart sat down in a chair across from us. ''Shall we talk about the job?''

I looked up from the magazines. ''We know you didn't advertise for two boys,'' I said. ''But we thought

12

maybe two of us working together would get it done faster. Whatever it is. Your ad didn't really say."

"Don't worry about that," she said, looking from one of us to the other. "I'm actually pleased that you both came. That way I can choose."

"Choose what?" I asked. "What do you mean?"

Mrs. Stewart had been staring at Simon intently, and she had an odd look on her face. When I spoke, she seemed to snap out of her spell. "Oh, I meant it gives me more choices for what jobs I can have done. There are so many, you know. With two of you, I can get *all* of them done."

"What exactly is the job?" I asked. "I mean, your house looks perfect."

Mrs. Stewart sighed. "There's so much to do," she said. "I just don't know where to start. You see, the attic and the basement are filled with old things. I need someone to help me sort through it all."

"We can do that," I said.

"Sure," said Simon. "I love to clean." I'd never seen Simon clean anything in his life. His room was a mess. I figured he was just trying to sell Mrs. Stewart on hiring us.

"Good," she said. "It will be so nice to have a boy around the house again. I mean, to have help around the house."

"So we're hired?" asked Simon.

Mrs. Stewart smiled at him. "Yes," she said. "I think you'll do just fine. Just fine indeed."

Simon grinned at me. "I told you we'd find the perfect jobs," he said.

Before I could answer, someone opened the door and began to call out.

"Martha? Martha, are you home?"

Mrs. Stewart looked up. "In here, James," she said.

A man walked into the living room. He was wearing a white suit and vest with a brightly flowered shirt. Around his neck was a heavy gold chain. His hair was combed back over his head. Like Mrs. Stewart, he seemed out of date, as though he'd just come from a costume party or something. The longer I looked at him, the more he reminded me of someone, but I couldn't quite remember who it was.

"James," Mrs. Stewart said. "This is Simon and Marshall. They're going to be helping me around the house."

Mr. Stewart came over and shook our hands. "Nice to meet you, boys." He seemed to be very nervous. When he took my hand, his skin was all clammy.

"Are you sure we need more boys, Martha?" he said. "Didn't you get all of that stuff taken care of last summer?"

Mrs. Stewart laughed. "Oh, James, you know that boy didn't work out." She turned to Simon and me. "I tried to get a boy last year, but he wasn't at all right. I finally had to let him go. Such a disappointment.''

"It's hard to find good help,'' I said.

"Yes,'' said Mrs. Stewart. "It really is. But I imagine the two of you are very good boys.''

Mr. Stewart cleared his throat. "Martha, do you really think this is a good—''

"James,'' Mrs. Stewart interrupted. "Why don't you have a Nehi and relax? Or maybe you need a nap.''

"No,'' Mr. Stewart said. "I don't need a nap. But I think a Nehi would be groovy—I mean great. I really don't think a nap is necessary.'' He went into the kitchen to get a drink.

Mrs. Stewart sighed. "James is under a lot of pressure,'' she said. "Sometimes I worry about him.''

"What does Mr. Stewart do?'' I asked.

"He teaches at the dance studio in town,'' she said. "He was quite a dancer in his day. You should have seen him boogying down on the floor.''

"Boogying?'' said Simon. "On the floor? Was something wrong with him?''

Mrs. Stewart looked at Simon. "You know, disco dancing,'' she said. "The hustle. The bump.'' Then she laughed. "I forget you kids today don't know about that stuff. Well, it was all the rage when Mr. Stewart and I were younger. We really used to kill them when we

15

got going. We were the Eerie disco champions four years running.''

She pointed to the ceiling. We looked up and saw that hanging in the middle of the room was a big ball covered in bits of mirrored glass. ''They gave us that after our third win,'' she said. ''Isn't it beautiful?''

''It sure is,'' said Simon.

''Do you still dance?'' I asked.

''Oh, no,'' Mrs. Stewart said. ''Not since . . . not for a long time now. I haven't really felt like it.'' She stood up. ''Well, boys. I have some errands to run in town. Why don't you come by first thing tomorrow morning and we'll get started?''

Mrs. Stewart showed us to the door.

''Thanks for the Nehi,'' I said.

''And the pigs in the blankets,'' added Simon.

''Oh, you're very welcome, boys. Remember, there's plenty more where that came from. I'm just so glad I found you. I know this is going to work out just fine. With both of you here, it will hardly take any time at all.''

She shut the door, and Simon and I walked back to our bikes.

''She sure is nice,'' said Simon. ''This job is going to be great.''

''It seems easy enough,'' I said. ''Maybe this won't be so bad after all. We can tell our dads that we got jobs, but it sounds like we'll still have a lot of free time.''

I wanted to believe that more than anything. But this was Eerie, where nothing is what it seems. As we pedaled down the driveway past the station wagon, I noticed that suddenly the Nehi and the pigs in the blankets just weren't sitting quite right in my stomach.

3

We showed up at the Stewarts' house the next morning. Mrs. Stewart was outside, planting pansies in the border around the house. She was tucking a clump of purple and blue ones into a pot carried by a ceramic garden gnome that stood beside the front steps. When she saw us, she stood and waved.

"Hello, boys," she called out, wiping dirt on her pink pants. "Ready to get started?"

"Sure," Simon said brightly. "Just show us what you need done."

Mrs. Stewart went into the house, and we followed her. "Why don't I give you the guided tour?" she said.

She led us down a hallway, pointing out the various rooms as we passed by. "There's the bathroom," she said, "and that's the rec room. Here's the dining room." It all looked perfectly ordinary to me, except that it was sort of out of date. I figured the Stewarts must not have much money for redecorating.

Mrs. Stewart walked up a flight of stairs to the second floor. "This is our bedroom," she said, waving to a doorway as we walked along behind her. "This room is my sewing room."

"What's that room over there?" Simon asked, pointing to a closed door next to the sewing room. Mrs. Stewart had walked right by it without saying anything.

Mrs. Stewart paused. "Oh," she said. "That's nothing to worry about. Just an extra room with a bunch of old things in it. You don't need to go in there. Now let's go take a look at the attic." She kept walking to the end of the hallway.

But there was something about the way she'd told us not to worry that made me do just the opposite. I wondered why she would keep that one room all closed up, when the rest were wide open. In my experience, when someone keeps a door shut, it's because there's something behind it they don't want anyone to see.

I looked down the hall. Mrs. Stewart was busy talking to Simon, and she didn't notice that I had lagged behind. Keeping my eye on her in case she turned around, I reached out and tried turning the knob on the door. It was locked.

I went and joined Simon and Mrs. Stewart at the end of the hall. "Sorry," I said. "I had to stop and tie my shoe."

Mrs. Stewart opened a door at the end of the hallway.

Some steps led up into the attic. "Now let's see. I know there's a light here somewhere," she said. "Ah, there it is."

She pulled a string hanging from the ceiling and a light came on. Then she went up the stairs, with Simon and I right behind her. The attic looked like any attic in any house. It was filled with piles of boxes and stuff that had probably been there for years.

"I'm afraid this place hasn't been cleaned out in a long time," Mrs. Stewart said. "You boys are going to have quite a bit of work to do."

"Look at all this cool stuff," Simon said. He was looking at a pile of old games and toys in one corner of the room. "How come you want to get rid of all of this?"

Mrs. Stewart sighed. "It's just been sitting here all these years with no one to play with it," she said sadly.

Simon picked up a baseball mitt and put it on. "Too bad," he said. "Someone could have a lot of fun with this stuff."

Mrs. Stewart walked over to where Simon was standing. She put her hand on his shoulder. "Maybe you'd like to keep some of these things, Simon," she said.

Simon looked up at her. "What? Me? You mean I could have this?"

Mrs. Stewart laughed. "Of course you can. Anything

you want. After all, I don't need it anymore, do I? Someone should get some use out of it."

She turned around and looked at me. "How about you, Marshall? Do you see anything here you like?"

The way she was staring at me made a chill run up and down my spine. It was as if she was testing me or something, like if I gave the wrong answer I'd flunk.

"Um, no thanks, Mrs. Stewart. I have enough stuff at home. My mom would kill me if I brought anything else into the house."

"Really," said Mrs. Stewart. "That's too bad."

"Good thing my mom never notices anything," said Simon. "She's so busy, sometimes I think she wouldn't even notice if I *disappeared*."

The smile on Mrs. Stewart's face got even bigger. "That's terrible," she said, putting her hand on Simon's shoulder again. "Such a shame."

"Maybe we should get started," I said. Something was bothering me about the way Mrs. Stewart was acting, and I wanted to be alone with Simon so I could talk to him about it.

"That's a good idea, Marshall," said Mrs. Stewart, although she didn't sound like she thought it was a good idea at all. "Here are some empty boxes. Why don't you boys start filling them up with that stuff over there. Then later on you can carry them out to the curb for the trash men to pick up."

She showed us which piles to start on, then headed back down the stairs. "I'll be back to check on you in an hour or so," she said as she left.

When she was gone, I sat down on a trunk. "Man, was she acting strange," I said to Simon.

He picked up a stack of old magazines and dropped them into the empty box. "What do you mean?"

"Didn't you see the way she was staring at you? It was like she was . . . inspecting you or something."

"I think she's just trying to be nice," said Simon.

"I don't know. Something just doesn't seem right about her. And I checked that door downstairs, too. It was locked."

"So, a lot of people keep rooms locked," Simon said. "What, do you think she has someone locked up in there or something?"

I laughed. "Okay, maybe you're right," I said. "I guess I'm just used to everything in this town being a little bit strange. And even if she *is* weird, she's keeping me from having to work with my dad."

I began sorting through a big pile of stuff, dividing it into smaller piles for throwing out. I couldn't believe how much junk there was in the Stewarts' attic. It was as if they'd saved everything they'd owned for the last twenty years. After a while I forgot all about Mrs. Stewart as I carried armloads of things from one part of the attic to the other.

22

I was dumping a whole bag of old shoes into the trash box when I heard the door open again and Mrs. Stewart came up the stairs.

"Hey, boys, want some lunch?" she called out.

I realized that I was starving. "I sure would," I said. I couldn't believe so much time had gone by so quickly.

"Me, too," agreed Simon. "I've moved so many magazines I could eat a horse."

"Would you settle for some sandwiches?" Mrs. Stewart said. "Come on down to the kitchen, and I'll make them up."

We all went back downstairs to the kitchen. Simon and I sat at the table while Mrs. Stewart made lunch. She was humming as she made the sandwiches, and there was something familiar about the tune.

"What's that song?" I asked. "I think I've heard it before."

"Oh, it's just something I used to sing," said Mrs. Stewart as she spread mayonnaise on the bread. "I don't think you'd know it. I hope you like olive loaf."

I made a face at Simon. "Olive loaf?" I mouthed. He shrugged.

Mrs. Stewart brought us our sandwiches and put them on the table. "And how about two big glasses of milk?" she asked, getting them before we could answer.

I took a bite of my sandwich and chewed slowly. It wasn't the worst thing I'd ever had, but it definitely wasn't a cheeseburger. When Mrs. Stewart sat down across from me, I tried to smile at her so she'd think I liked the food. But she was more interested in Simon.

"So, Simon," she said. "Tell me more about yourself. Do you have any brothers and sisters?"

"Nope," Simon said, his mouth full of olive loaf. "It's just me."

"I have a sister," I said.

"That's nice," Mrs. Stewart said without looking at me. "What kinds of things do you like to do, Simon?"

Simon shrugged. "I don't know," he said. "I like a lot of stuff. You know—baseball, video games, comic books. The usual."

Mrs. Stewart seemed to be thinking about something. "Video games," she said finally. "I'm pretty sure we still have an Atari in the rec room. Maybe you'd like to play it sometime. I think we have Pac-Man."

"Pac-Man?" Simon said. "They haven't made that game for about a billion years."

Mrs. Stewart frowned. "Well, we've had this for quite some time now. My . . . Mr. Stewart likes to play it."

She watched us as we ate in silence, smiling the whole time. She was making me really nervous. "Would you like another sandwich?" she asked when we finished. "There's plenty more."

"No, thanks," Simon answered. "I think we should get back to work. This was great, though."

We got up and went back to the attic as Mrs. Stewart cleared the plates away. As we walked down the hall, I heard her humming again.

"I know I've heard that song before," I said. "I just can't remember where."

"It's probably something that's been on the radio," Simon suggested. "That happens to me all the time. Last week I kept hearing the new Oyster Jelly song in my head. It made me nuts until I remembered what it was."

"Maybe you're right," I said. "I'll probably remember it later."

Back in the attic, we continued to sort through the piles of junk. As I was putting some old ice skates into one of the boxes, something occurred to me.

"Hey, don't you think it's weird that the Stewarts don't have any kids?" I said. "I mean, look at all of this old sports equipment up here. Someone had to have used it. And why would they have video games if they didn't have a kid?"

"Maybe they do have one," Simon said. "But he's all grown up now and this is his stuff."

"No," I said. "She looks too young to have a grown-up kid. Besides, there would be pictures of him on the wall or the refrigerator or something. You know how moms are. There isn't anything like that around."

"I don't know," said Simon. "Maybe they just collect sports equipment. You're too suspicious. Let's just get this stuff boxed up."

With all of the moving around, it was starting to get really stuffy in the room, and the air was filled with flying dust. I inhaled some and sneezed. As I did, I accidentally knocked over another box that was sitting on top of the pile. The lid fell off, and a bunch of papers slid out onto the floor.

"Oh, great, something else to clean up," I said.

Simon and I knelt down to pick up the mess. It seemed to be a pile of drawings done by a little kid. The top one showed a house with a man and a woman standing in front of it.

"Hey, that looks like this house," I said, pointing to the red squiggles under the windows. "Those are the flower boxes."

"And that guy is wearing a white suit," Simon added. "Just like the one Mr. Stewart wears."

"That must be Mrs. Stewart," I said. "See, she's wearing pink pants."

"But who's that?" asked Simon. Standing between the two big figures was a smaller one. It looked like a boy wearing a red shirt.

"I don't know," I said. "Let's look at the rest of them."

A lot of the drawings were of the same house. Some of them had people in them. One had a black dog. The same boy in the red shirt appeared in three or four of the pictures.

I picked up the last drawing. It showed the boy lying in what looked like a big box. The dog was curled up next to him, and the woman from the other pictures was putting something over them. She was smiling, but the boy wasn't.

"What's she doing?" Simon said.

"It looks like she's tucking him into bed," I said. "But it doesn't look quite right. It looks more like she's putting him in a box or something."

I started to put the pictures down when something else fell out and fluttered to the floor. I picked it up. It was a photograph of a boy.

"Hey, that's the kid in the pictures," Simon exclaimed. "See, he's even wearing the same red shirt. So he *is* real."

I looked closely at the photo. The boy looked as though he was about Simon's age. He appeared to be at his birthday party. He was taking the top off of a box, and a puppy was sticking its head out and licking the boy's face. Around the puppy's neck there was a big red bow.

"And I bet that's the dog," I said.

"But who is it?" asked Simon.

"I have no idea. But he looks a lot like you, doesn't he?"

Simon picked up the photo. "Sort of," he said. "We have the same color hair."

"If that *is* the Stewarts in those drawings," I said, "and the kid in the drawing is the same kid in the picture, then who is he and what was he doing with them?"

Before we could continue talking, I heard the door to the attic open and someone start to come up the stairs.

"Oh, boys," called Mrs. Stewart. "How are things going up here?"

"Quick," I whispered to Simon, "put the pictures back in the box." I didn't want Mrs. Stewart to think we'd been snooping through her stuff.

We managed to get everything put away before she reached the top of the stairs. When she got there, we were putting the last of the old magazines into a pile.

"Hi," I said. "We're almost done with these."

She looked around the room. "Well, you're moving very quickly," she said. "Why don't you take these boxes down to the trash and we'll call it a day. I'm sure you boys have something more exciting to do with the rest of your afternoon."

Simon and I carried the boxes down the stairs and

out to the curb. When we were done, we said good-bye to Mrs. Stewart.

"I'll see you tomorrow after school," she said.

"I can't wait," I said.

"Me neither," added Simon.

We got on our bikes and started to pedal home. When I was sure we were out of sight, I reached into my shirt pocket and took out the photo I'd hidden there. I looked at the boy and his dog. I didn't know who they were, but I had a terrible feeling I was going to find out pretty soon, and that I wouldn't like the answer.

4

That night after dinner, Simon and I reconvened in the Secret Spot. Okay, so it's really just the attic, but it's still secret. It's where we keep all the proof of the weird stuff we've uncovered in Eerie. And we have a lot. We have boxes of photographs we've taken, and maps of the whole town with the centers of strangeness circled. There's also a trunk filled with evidence, like the plaster cast we made of the Bigfoot prints we found in Simon's backyard, the bandages from the mummy we uncovered last year, and the silver bullet we used to stop the Eerie werewolf. I also keep my journal up there, hidden away in a locked drawer so no one who might be snooping around can find it. I write down *everything* that happens to us, so in case anything—you know—fatal, ever happens to me and Simon, there will be a record of the weirdness in Eerie. Not that anyone would believe it.

So there we were, ready to investigate the latest

Eerie mystery. Once we made sure that the door was locked and no one could bother us, I pulled down the shades, took out the picture of the kid and his dog, and started to examine it closely for clues. On the surface, it looked like any ordinary photo of a boy at his birthday party. But I knew if we looked hard enough we'd find something else, something out of the ordinary.

After five minutes, I hadn't found anything useful. I just kept staring at the kid's smiling face and the dog with its tongue hanging out and the bow around its neck. They both looked perfectly happy, as though nothing bad had happened to them in their lives. I was at a dead end.

"This is useless," I said, throwing the picture down on my desk. "For all we know, this is just the Stewarts' nephew or something."

"Maybe whoever took it wrote something on the back," suggested Simon. "You know, like the kid's name or something. My mom is always taking pictures and writing descriptions of what they're of on the backs. She drags them out whenever my grandparents come to visit. She even has one of me naked in the bathtub when I was five. It's embarrassing."

Sometimes the most obvious solution is the one that seems too easy to be true. I picked the photograph up and turned it over. There was nothing written on it about who the kid was, but down in one corner there was a date printed on the paper in blue ink.

"Summer, 1976," it said.

Simon let out a whoop. "Yes! Our first real lead. Now we know when it was taken."

"But who is it?" I said. "And why was that box of drawings in the Stewarts' attic?" We had a clue, but it was a small one.

I turned the photo back over and scanned the front again. The way the picture was shot, you couldn't really tell where the boy was having his party. His face and the dog's were in sharp focus, but the background was all kind of fuzzy. He could have been in any house in any town.

"This is hopeless," I said, putting the picture back down on my desk. "There's no way we'll be able to tell who this kid is."

"Wait a minute," Simon said, picking up the picture and staring at it. "What's this?"

"What's what?"

"This thing on the side," he said. "There's something in the picture, but it's been cut off by the edge so you only see a little piece of it."

I took the picture and looked at it again. Simon was right. Over the boy's shoulder, there was something hanging on the wall. I could see the outline of it, but it was hard to tell what it was.

"Hand me the magnifying glass," I told Simon. "Maybe that will help."

Simon gave me the magnifying glass, and I held it over the picture. Under the glass, the boy's head looked huge, and the puppy's face was all distorted. But it also made everything in the background a little clearer. I could see that there were kitchen cabinets on the wall behind the table where the boy was sitting.

I moved the glass over the spot that Simon had pointed out. It was still blurry, but I could see now that it was something black. There was a long thin thing hanging down from the bottom, and the top was round.

"I have no idea what this is," I said.

Simon took the magnifying glass and looked at the picture.

"It's a clock," he said.

"A clock? That thing? That doesn't look like any clock I've ever seen."

"It is," said Simon. "It's shaped like a cat. The top is its head. See the pointy things on the sides? Those are its ears. And that long thing is its tail. It moves back and forth, counting the seconds. It also has a tongue that sticks out every hour."

"How do you know all this?" I asked.

Simon put the magnifying glass down. "Because I saw one just like this the other day. I remember thinking how creepy it looked. It was all covered with rhine-stones, and it had big white eyes.''

"You saw one?'' I said. "Where?''

Simon looked at me. "In the Stewarts' kitchen. I saw it while we were eating lunch. It was behind you, so you didn't see it.''

"So this picture was taken in the Stewarts' kitchen,'' I said. "That's one more piece of the puzzle solved.''

"Okay,'' said Simon, "so now we know the picture was taken in the Stewarts' house in the summer of 1976. We still don't know who the kid is or where he is now. For all we know, it was just some ordinary birthday party and we're making a big deal out of nothing.''

"I don't think so,'' I said. "Why would the same kid be in all of those drawings if he wasn't connected to the Stewarts? There's something they're hiding.''

"Yeah, but what is it?'' said Simon.

"Don't worry,'' I said, "we'll find out. Tomorrow we're going to search that attic for more clues.''

When we arrived at the Stewarts' house right after school on Monday, we pretended that everything was fine. I didn't want them to think we were up to anything, or that we were suspicious of what else might be hidden in their attic. When Mr. Stewart offered us a snack, I said we had a lot more to do in the attic, and Simon and I hurried up there.

"Okay," I said when we were back among the dusty boxes and piles of old clothes, "It's time to look for clues. Try to find anything that might help us figure out who the kid in the picture is."

Simon started rummaging through a heap of boxes, while I went back to the place where we'd found the stack of drawings. I'd left them sitting right on top of the box they'd fallen out of, but now they were gone.

"Hey, Simon," I called. "Did you take the drawings and put them somewhere else?"

"No. I didn't touch them," he answered. "Why?"

"They're gone," I said. "And I know I left them right here. She must have taken them."

"Who?" asked Simon.

"Her. Mrs. Stewart. She must not have wanted us to see them."

"Why would she care?"

"I don't know," I said. "There's something she's trying to hide. I just know it."

Simon opened another box. "Hey, come look at this," he said.

I went over and peered into the box. It was filled with photo albums, the kind with nature pictures on the covers that you get at any drugstore. I picked one up and opened it. On the first page was a picture of Mrs. Stewart. She looked very young, and she was holding a baby in her arms. She was smiling and waving at the camera.

I turned the pages. Each one was filled with pictures of Mrs. and Mr. Stewart and the baby. Some showed them holding it; others showed the baby sitting playing with blocks or just smiling at nothing. There was even one of the baby opening a present at Christmas. Mr. Stewart was helping it, and he was wearing a bow on his head like a hat.

I took out the next album and opened it. It, too, was filled with pictures of the Stewarts and the baby. Only now the baby was bigger, and you could tell that it was a boy. He was walking around and laughing. I opened another album, then another, flipping quickly through the pages. As I looked at picture after picture of the boy, I could see him getting older. By the time I got to the fifth album, I could tell that the kid in the pictures looked a lot like the one in the photograph hidden in my desk.

I reached into the box and took out the next-to-last album. The pictures in that one were much more recent than the first ones. The boy had grown up a lot. In one of the pictures, he was standing with a dog in a yard. The dog had a yellow ball in his mouth, and the boy was reaching for it.

"It's him," I said. "It's the kid. And that's the dog from the picture."

Simon whistled. "So, the Stewarts *did* have a kid," he said. "I wonder what happened to him."

"I don't know," I said, "but I'm sure it's something weird. Why else would all of these pictures be hidden up here?"

"Maybe there's something in that last album," suggested Simon.

He reached in and pulled out the final album. He flipped it open and looked at the pictures. Like the last album, this one also had pictures of a birthday. Lots of pictures.

"That kid had a lot of birthdays," I said.

"But it's not the same kid," said Simon, holding out the album. "Look, they're all different kids."

I took the album and looked more closely. Simon was right. Each page held photographs of a birthday, but the boys were all different.

"They all look sort of like that kid," I said. "And look, each one of them is opening the same box with a puppy in it."

Sure enough, the pictures were almost identical. In each one, a kid was opening a box and a puppy with a red bow around its neck was poking its head out. In fact, except for the different kids, it could have been the same picture over and over again.

Only the first four pages had pictures on them. The

rest were empty. I shut the book and put it back in the box.

"This gets weirder and weirder," I said. "Who were all those kids?"

"And why are they all having the same party?" said Simon. "It doesn't make any sense."

"Maybe they're brothers?" I suggested, but even I knew that was ridiculous. There had been only one kid in all the other albums. Suddenly there were five or six different ones. Where had they come from? Instead of answers, we were just turning up more questions.

"So what do we do now?" asked Simon.

I thought for a minute. "Nothing," I said. "We just have to wait and see what else we can find out. In the meantime, we'd better get back to work. We don't want Mrs. Stewart to come up here and see us doing nothing."

For the next hour, we filled boxes with junk and carried them downstairs. Every time I passed the kitchen on my way to take the trash out, I looked at the cat clock on the wall and shuddered as I wondered what had happened to the kids in the pictures.

If Mrs. Stewart knew that we had found the drawings in the attic, she never let on. If anything, she was nicer to us than ever before. She brought us lemonade, and for a snack she made hamburgers with melted cheese on them.

"Eat up!" she said as she emptied a bag of potato chips into a bowl and set it on the table.

I took a handful of chips and put them on my plate. "This burger is great, Mrs. Stewart," I said. "You're a wonderful cook."

"Why thank you, Marshall," she said. "How about you, Simon? Do you like yours?"

Simon swallowed a big bite. "I sure do," he said. "These are even better than the burgers at Burger Chef."

Mrs. Stewart seemed pleased that we liked her food, and I decided the time was right to take a risk. "It's too bad you don't have any kids," I said to her. "If you did, I bet they'd love your cooking."

Mrs. Stewart looked down at the plate she was washing in the sink. "Yes," she said, "it is too bad, isn't it? Maybe someday I will have a little boy. A little boy who loves hamburgers as much as you and Simon do. That would be wonderful. Just like I'd always dreamed."

She was smiling a strange smile as she stared at the sudsy water in the sink. It was as though she was thinking hard about something. Suddenly she started humming. It was the same song I'd heard her humming the day before, and again it sounded familiar. I just couldn't remember why.

Then, just as suddenly as she'd started, Mrs. Stewart

stopped humming. She rinsed the dish in her hand and put it in the drainer. Then she dried her hands on her apron.

"Well, it's time for me to take a little beauty nap," she said. "I'll just leave you boys to finish your snack. Don't forget to put your dishes in the sink before you go back to work."

"We won't," I said.

The rest of the afternoon turned up nothing interesting. No matter how many boxes we looked through, we couldn't find any other clues about who the kids in the pictures were. We did, however, carry dozens of boxes out to the curb, and by the time five o'clock rolled around, we were more than ready to go.

Going back downstairs, we said good-bye to Mrs. Stewart. She had taken a nap, and she seemed to be in a very good mood. She was in the living room listening to some records and dancing around.

"Hey there, boys," she said. "Like the music?"

I didn't, but I said I did. "Are you practicing for a dance contest?" I asked, remembering what she had said about her and Mr. Stewart having been dancers.

"Oh, no," she said. "I just felt like hearing some of the old songs again. They make me feel so young."

"Okay," I said, watching her dance around the room. "Well, we're going to go now."

We were just about to leave when a small black dog

came running into the room, followed closely by Mr. Stewart.

"Spike!" he called. "Spike, come back here."

"James!" Mrs. Stewart shrieked. "What is he doing out?"

"I thought he might like a walk," Mr. Stewart said. "I'm sorry. He's been inside for so long. I'll put him back."

The dog ran up to Simon and jumped up on him, licking his face. Mr. Stewart grabbed the dog by the collar and dragged him out of the room.

"I didn't know you had a dog," I said.

Mrs. Stewart laughed nervously. "Oh, yes," she said. "That's Spike. We've had him a long time."

"That's funny," said Simon. "He acts like a puppy."

"He can be very fresh," said Mrs. Stewart. "That's why we keep him in his room. So, we'll see you tomorrow then."

All of a sudden she seemed anxious for us to go. As we were going out the door, I remembered something.

"I have a dentist appointment tomorrow," I told Mrs. Stewart, "so I'll be a little late. I hope that's okay."

"That's fine," said Mrs. Stewart. "Simon, you'll still be coming at the usual time, right?"

"Sure thing, Mrs. Stewart."

She beamed. "Well then, that's absolutely perfect."

We left the Stewarts and rode home.

"Did something seem weird about Spike?" I asked Simon.

"You mean that he looked exactly like the dog in the picture?" he said.

"Right," I said. "I bet he's one of that other dog's puppies."

"Which makes this whole thing even weirder," said Simon. "Tomorrow we'll have to expand our search."

"And tomorrow is when your parents leave, right?"

"Right," said Simon. His parents were going to visit his mother's sister in Normal, Illinois, for a week, and Simon was going to stay at our house.

"You sure you'll be okay alone there, at the Stewarts'?" I asked.

"No problem," Simon said. "What could possibly happen in an hour or two?"

As it turned out—a lot could happen.

5

*F*or a change, my visit to the dentist wasn't all that bad. I'd gotten a retainer the year before, and I usually remembered to wear it. All Dr. Payne did was clean my teeth and tell me I should floss more regularly. After getting a brand-new green toothbrush, I was free to go join Simon at the Stewarts.' I was anxious to resume our search for clues, so I rode over there as fast as I could.

As I parked my bike near the garage, I was surprised not to see Simon's bike anywhere. I figured that for some reason he must have walked over. I went up to the front door and rang the bell. As I waited for someone to answer, I noticed that the front windows all had the shades drawn. It seemed strange, especially since it was bright and sunny out, but so many things about the Stewarts were strange that I didn't worry too much about it.

When no one answered the door I rang again, holding the buzzer down for a longer time. Finally, I saw one of the curtains open and Mrs. Stewart's face peer out. She didn't look happy to see me standing on her porch. Then the curtain closed again, and I heard someone fumbling with the door. It sounded as though a lot of locks were being opened.

The door opened a crack and Mrs. Stewart stuck her head out.

"Hi," I said. "Is Simon here yet?"

Mrs. Stewart shook her head. "No," she said. "He never showed up today." She kept looking over my shoulder, scanning the street.

"That's weird," I said. "It's not like him to be late."

There was a crash from inside the house. Mrs. Stewart looked behind her, then turned back to me. "Well, he didn't come," she said quickly. "Now, if you'll excuse me, I really have to . . ."

"But don't you want me to work?" I interrupted. "We've only cleaned out a little bit of the attic, and there's a ton of stuff still up there."

She was shutting the door quickly. "No," she said through the rapidly shrinking crack. "I don't think we'll be needing you boys anymore. Thank you. Good-bye."

The door slammed shut, and I heard more clicking sounds as Mrs. Stewart locked it again. Then I heard another crash, as if something had fallen over and broken. I rang the bell again.

"What is it?" said Mrs. Stewart when she opened the door again. This time she sounded angry.

"I'm sorry to bother you again," I said. "But you didn't pay us for the days we worked."

Mrs. Stewart frowned. "Just a minute," she said. The door shut again, and I heard her moving around in the living room. When she reappeared, she had some bills in her hand. She shoved them at me through the crack and I took them.

"Thanks," I said. "I'm sorry you won't need us anymore. I know Simon was really enjoying working here. Are you sure you haven't seen him?"

"No," said Mrs. Stewart. "I mean, yes, I'm sure I haven't seen him. Now, good-bye."

From inside the house I heard more noises, as though someone was rolling around on the floor.

"Is everything okay?" I asked.

"It's fine," said Mrs. Stewart. "It's just . . . Spike . . . making a mess. I have to go see to it."

This time when she shut the door I knew I wouldn't be able to get her to open it again. Whatever was going on in there, Mrs. Stewart didn't want me to see it. I folded up the money she'd given me and put it in my pocket. It was time to go find Simon and see why he hadn't shown up at the Stewarts' house. It seemed as

45

though we were never going to solve the mystery of the kids in the pictures, after all.

First I rode over to Simon's house. His parents were already gone on their trip, and the front door was locked. I knew where they hid the spare key inside their mail box, though, so I got it and went inside.

"Simon?" I yelled as I went up the stairs to his room. "Hey, Simon."

I threw open the door to his room. "Hey, Mrs. Stewart said that she doesn't—"

Simon's room was empty. At the foot of his bed was a small bag with some clothes in it. It was the bag he was supposed to pick up after school to bring to my house later on that evening.

I checked the bathroom next, but it was empty, too, except for a wet towel on the floor. In fact, the whole house was empty. In the kitchen I found a plate and glass in the sink, so I guessed that Simon had gone home and eaten a snack after school. But where had he gone then?

I went back outside and opened the garage door. The Holmes's station wagon was gone. So was Simon's bike. That meant he'd left, as he was supposed to. But for some reason, he'd never made it to the Stewarts' house. Something—or someone—had stopped him before he could get there.

I decided to retrace Simon's tracks. If he'd gone the

way we usually went, then *someone* had to have seen him go by. I hopped on my bike and started off.

I drove by World of Stuff. Mr. Radford was outside sweeping the sidewalk.

"Hey, Mr. Radford," I said. "Did you happen to see Simon ride by here this afternoon?"

Mr. Radford leaned on his broom and thought. "Simon?" he said.

I sighed. Mr. Radford was always forgetting things. "You know," I said. "The kid who's always with me. About this high. Brown hair. Baseball cap. He likes the *Bizarre Files* comics."

Mr. Radford brightened. "Oh, *Simon*," he said. "Right."

I waited for him to continue, but he just kept smiling at me.

"Well?"

He looked puzzled. "Well what?"

"Did you see Simon?" I said impatiently.

"Oh, um, yes, I guess I did. On Saturday, right? You boys came in for hot fudge sundaes. No nuts."

I sighed. "No, not Saturday. Today."

"You came in for sundaes today? Where was I?"

"No!" I shouted. "No, we had sundaes on Saturday. Did you see him today?"

"Not if you came in on Saturday," Mr. Radford said.

47

"How could I? You aren't making any sense, young man."

I gave up. "Thanks, Mr. Radford. I'll see you later."

I continued down the street until I came to "The King's" house. The King looks just like Elvis Presley, the famous singer who supposedly died but who everyone says is still alive. In fact, I think he *is* Elvis Presley and he's hiding out in Eerie so everyone will leave him alone. But he insists that we just call him The King. He lives on my paper route, so I see him all the time.

Anyway, The King was outside watering his lawn. As usual, he had on dark sunglasses and his hair was greased back. He had on a blue outfit covered in thousands of rhinestones that glittered in the light. He was singing to himself as he waved the hose over the grass.

"Hey, there, little paper boy," he said when I stopped at the curb. He always calls me "little paper boy."

"Hey, King," I said. "Have you seen Simon around?"

The King put his hand on his chin and thought for a minute. "Can't say as I have, little paper boy. But then, I just got up, so I haven't seen much. Me and Marilyn were up late last night watching the stars. There was a blue moon, you know."

Marilyn was The King's neighbor. As if on cue, she opened her screen door and came outside. She was wearing the same white dress she always wore. Her blonde hair was perfectly done up, and her lips were bright red.

"Ooh," she said when she saw me. "Who's this?"

"It's the little paper boy," The King said.

"Ooh," Marilyn said again.

"I'm looking for a friend of mine," I said.

"A friend?" she said. "What kind of friend?"

"A kid," I said. "Riding a bike. He should have gone by here about three hours ago. Did you see him?"

"Not me," she said, shaking her head.

"Okay," I said. "Thanks anyway."

The King pointed at me. "No, thank you, little paper boy. Don't be cruel, now, you hear? Wouldn't want you to get all shook up over this."

The King was always saying weird stuff like that. I just waved and rode off.

I stopped at every house along the street. No one had seen Simon ride by. I was starting to think it was hopeless to even try to look for him. It was as though he'd just vanished into thin air. Then, when I reached the traffic light, I saw a police car. Sitting in the front seat was Chief Hoffa. He and his family lived in the creepy old house by the cemetery, and he'd been the head of the Eerie Police for as long as anyone could remember. He knew everything that went on there. Or at least he thought he did.

I rode over to his car. "Hey, Chief Hoffa," I said.

"So, what can I do for you this fine morning?" he asked.

"Well, it's Simon," I said. "I can't find him anywhere."

"Think the UFOs got him?" Chief Hoffa said. Then he chuckled. Simon and I had reported spotting some UFOs once, but Chief Hoffa hadn't believed us.

"Good one," I said, pretending to laugh at his joke. "No, I don't know where he is. You haven't seen him today, have you?"

Chief Hoffa opened a little notebook he kept in his shirt pocket. He scanned the page.

"Let's see," he said. "Seven A.M. Saw one red van pull up outside World of Stuff. Man unloaded boxes marked EXPLOSIVES. That wouldn't be your friend, would it?"

"No," I said. "Simon doesn't drive. He's only eleven."

"Hmmm. How about this: Eight-thirty A.M. Woman in clown suit chasing kite down the street. Sound familiar?"

"No," I said again. "He would have been riding his bike. And anyway it would be later, right after school."

Chief Hoffa looked again. "Ah, here we go," he said. "Two forty-five. Spotted one boy on a bicycle riding down Earhart Road. Looked suspicious. I would have followed him, but I hadn't finished my coffee and doughnut. Meant to look into it later."

"That's him," I said. "That was at two-forty-five? Are you sure?"

Chief Hoffa stared at me. "Am I sure? Young man, I am a police officer. It's my duty to keep my eyes open for anything odd going on in this town. I think I recognize suspicious characters when I see them."

"I'm sure you do," I said. "Thanks. Thanks a lot."

I left Chief Hoffa and sped toward Earhart Road. That was the shortcut we took to get to the Stewarts' house. If Simon had been spotted there, it meant that he'd been on his way as he was supposed to be. But according to Mrs. Stewart, he hadn't shown up. Something wasn't right.

I turned onto Earhart and rode slowly, scanning the area for signs of Simon. When I got to the end of the block, I hadn't found or seen anything unusual. I decided then that I should try going back to the Stewarts' house one more time. Maybe Simon had shown up later and was still there. At least I could ask Mrs. Stewart if she'd seen him since I left.

When I turned into their driveway, I saw Mr. Stewart getting out of their car. I waved to him.

"Hey, Mr. Stewart. I was just wondering, did Simon come by here? I've been looking all over for him, but no one's seen him."

Mr. Stewart leaned up against the car. He seemed surprised to see me.

"Um, let me think," he said. "Well now, I seem to recall that he did show up."

"Great," I said. "Is he still here?"

"No . . . uh . . . no, he isn't here right now," said Mr. Stewart. He kept biting his lip and glancing toward the house. He was sweating a lot. "He's gone. I mean, he left."

"Did he say where he was going?"

"No, I don't think he did. Just got on his bike and rode off. Said he had something to do. Somewhere to go. Someone to meet. Something like that."

"What time was he here?"

"Oh, you know, the usual time. Right at three. Very punctual boy."

"Wait a minute," I said. "Mrs. Stewart told me he never showed up. But if he was here at three, she would have seen him, wouldn't she?"

"Oh, did she say that?" Mr. Stewart had turned very pale, and he was sweating more than ever. "Well, she must be right, then."

"But you just said you saw him . . ."

"I must be mistaken," he said. "Happens all the time. Now, if you'll excuse me, I have to go. I'm very busy."

He turned around and started to walk very quickly toward the house. He looked back twice to see if I was still there, so I got on my bike and started to ride away. When he saw me leave, he went into the house and shut the door behind him.

I rode around the corner and stopped. I walked my bike behind a group of trees and parked it where no one could see it from the road. Then I sat down and tried to think. I knew now that Simon *had* gone to the Stewarts'. For some reason, Mrs. Stewart had lied to me about seeing him. And now Mr. Stewart was acting all funny. Nothing was adding up.

I decided to check out the Stewarts' house. There was something they weren't telling me. Leaving my bike hidden by the trees, I walked back toward the house, being careful to stay on the side where they wouldn't be able to see me if they happened to look out their windows. Checking to make sure the coast was clear, I ran quickly along the side of the garage.

I started to creep toward the back of the house. But as I passed the garage windows, something caught my eye and made me stop. Something bright orange. Looking inside, I saw a bike leaning up against one of the walls. The orange thing I'd seen was a safety flag attached to the back fender. I looked more closely. There was something very familiar about that bike.

It was Simon's.

*F*or a minute I just stood there staring at the bike, telling myself that it couldn't possibly be Simon's, that it had to be some kind of coincidence. But the more I looked, the more I knew that it was true. Simon was the only kid in Eerie with a bike like that. He'd painted it bright red with blue stripes on it, and there was a big sticker on the back that said I BRAKE FOR VAMPIRES. He'd put it on there after our run-in with . . . Well, never mind, that's a whole other story. Just believe me when I tell you that *no one* else had a sticker, or a bike, like that.

Once I accepted that it was Simon's bike, my next concern was about what I should do. What I *wanted* to do was run straight back to Chief Hoffa and have him break down the Stewarts' door and demand to know where Simon was. And in any other town, that's exactly what I would have done. But this was Eerie, where nothing was normal, not even the police. I knew that if I told Chief Hoffa that I thought something had happened to Simon, he'd just tell me I was imagining things, or insist that Simon was playing a joke on me. The same with my parents. They never believed me when I told them the weird things I knew about Eerie. No, I was on my own. I had to take care of finding Simon myself.

If Simon's bike was in the garage, then I knew he couldn't be too far away. I didn't know why the Stewarts had lied to me about him, or what had really happened between two-forty-five and three o'clock that afternoon, but I was sure that the answer was inside that house. I walked as quickly as I could toward the house, trying to stay out of sight. The closer I got, the more scared I became. If the Stewarts did have Simon in there, there was no telling what they were up to.

I reached the back of the house and flattened myself against the wall. Inching my way around, I headed for the nearest window. I hoped that I would be able to see something that would help me find Simon and get out of there as quickly as possible before anyone saw me.

When I reached the window, I took a deep breath and looked inside. All I saw was blackness. The shades had been pulled down and the curtains were drawn. It was like looking into the night sky. I moved to the next window and tried again. Same thing—nothing. In fact, every window I came to was blocked, just like the windows in the front of the house had been.

Whatever the Stewarts were up to, they didn't want anyone to know about it. I'd covered two sides of the house without finding anything. Because it was daylight, I couldn't risk trying the front of the house again. I was just about to double back and check the garage again for clues when I heard the front door to the house open. Ducking down behind a bush, I waited to see what was happening.

Mr. Stewart came out onto the front steps. Mrs. Stewart followed him.

"And don't forget to pick up some soda and some party hats," she was saying. "I want this to be perfect, James. Not like last time."

"Yes, dear," said Mr. Stewart. He was looking all around him, as though he was searching for something. Or watching out for something.

"Stop being so nervous," said Mrs. Stewart. "No one saw anything. It's fine. I've got him up in his room. He's taking a nice long nap."

Mr. Stewart wiped his forehead. "I don't feel good about this, Martha," he said. "I thought you said the last time really was the last time."

"James," Mrs. Stewart said sternly. "I haven't searched all these years for nothing. Now go get the things I asked for and hurry home. We have a lot of work to do before tomorrow.''

"But what if that other boy—''

"He won't be a problem, James. I told you, I took care of him, right after I put Simon—I mean Rodney— down for his nap.''

I gasped. So she *had* kidnapped Simon. But why was she calling him Rodney?

"Did you hear something?'' Mr. Stewart said. He was looking over toward the bushes where I was hiding. My heart was beating wildly as I waited for him to come and investigate.

"No,'' said Mrs. Stewart. "I did not hear anything. Now, go.''

Mr. Stewart gave the bushes another look, but he didn't come over. Instead, he got into the car, started it, and drove away. Mrs. Stewart went back inside the house and shut the door. I sat down behind the bush and thought. Now I knew that the Stewarts had kidnapped Simon. But again, I didn't know *why* they would do something like that. Why would they want to take a kid and keep him locked up in their house? Was it connected to the pictures in the attic? And what did she mean about a nap? I knew Simon would never put up with taking a nap. Not unless she'd done something to him.

I needed more information. I had a couple of pieces

of the puzzle, but the whole picture just wasn't coming together. There had to be a way to make it all fit, if I could just find the key I needed. I tried to think of everything I knew about the Stewarts. I had the picture of the kid whose name I didn't know, and the other pictures of other kids. I knew Mr. Stewart taught dance downtown. I knew that he and Mrs. Stewart had won some dance trophies a long time ago. But that was about it. None of it explained why they would want to take Simon hostage.

That's when it came to me. If the Stewarts had won some awards, there might have been something about it in the town newspaper. If I could find the articles, I might be able to get some more information about them. Information that would help me find out what was going on and help me get Simon back.

Doubling back around the house and the garage, I retrieved my bike from its hiding spot and headed for the town library. When I got there, I ran inside and rushed over to the front desk. Mr. Poe, the librarian, was sitting behind it writing furiously in a notebook. When he saw me, he looked up.

"Ah," he said. "What rhymes with 'nevermore'?"

"I don't know," I said. "How about 'candy store'? Can you tell me where I would find old issues of the *Eerie Examiner*?"

"Around the corner," he said, going back to writing in his book. "Arranged by year."

"Thanks," I said, and left. As I turned the corner, I heard him muttering to himself, "Rapping at the candy store? No, no, that just won't do. I'll have to ask Lenore for help." Crazy old guy.

I found the newspaper section and started scanning the rows. Each year was bound together in several big books, so all I had to do was pick which one I wanted. The problem was that I had no idea what year the Stewarts had won the dance championships.

Then I remembered the date on the magazines on the coffee table and on the photograph: summer, 1976. There seemed to be something special about that year. It was all I had to go on, but it would have to do. I found the row of papers from 1976 and took out the July–August issue. Carrying it over to one of the big tables, I sat down and opened it.

It was weird looking at the old papers. There were ads for products I'd never even heard of, and for movies I'd only seen on videotape. I felt as though I was opening up a time capsule from more than twenty years ago. It was so much fun looking that I almost forgot why I was there.

One ad in particular caught my eye. It was for a movie called *Saturday Night Fever*. There was a picture of a man on a dance floor. He was wearing a white suit exactly like the one Mr. Stewart was wearing. When I saw it, I knew I was on the right track.

I flipped quickly through the pages, looking for any mention of the Stewarts. There didn't seem to be anything. Then I turned a page and saw the headline: LOCAL COUPLE WINS FOURTH DISCO COMPETITION. Beneath it was a short article.

July 04

James and Martha Stewart won first prize at the annual Eerie Boogie-Down this past Saturday night. The couple, who have won top honors for the last four years in a row, wowed the audience with their combination of hip-shaking grooves and snappy footwork.

"We just can't stop dancing!" exclaimed Martha, who stole the night in her red satin stretch pants, tube top, and chiffon scarf.

"Eerie is such a happening place," added James, who managed to stay cool in his three-piece white suit as he twirled his wife around the floor.

When asked whether or not they would compete for a fifth time, Martha said, laughing. "We could dance *forever*," she said. And from the way they moved last night, they just might.

Alongside the article was a picture of Mr. and Mrs. Stewart. When I saw it, I couldn't believe my eyes. They looked exactly the same as they did now, right down to the white suit Mr. Stewart had on and the blue eye shadow that circled Mrs. Stewart's eyes. It was as if they'd just stepped out of the photo and into the real world. They hadn't aged a day in over twenty years.

7

For several minutes I just stared at the picture, taking in all the details. Above the Stewarts' heads hung a big glitter ball, just like the one in their living room. Mr. Stewart had on the same gold chain he was wearing when I first saw him. Mrs. Stewart had on the same shoes she'd been wearing when Simon and I found her dancing in the living room. It was like looking at a picture taken that morning, only it was from 1976.

I looked around to make sure that no one was watching, then I carefully tore out the picture and the article and folded it into a square. I stuck it in my pocket and put the book of newspapers back on the shelf. Then, as I was turning around to leave, something made me decide to look through some of the other volumes. I thought I might find something else useful.

The September–October volume was missing, so I picked up the November–December volume and started looking through it. It was strange, reading about what was happening in Eerie back then. I scanned each page, taking it all in. WORLD OF STUFF HAS ANNUAL GOING-OUT-OF-BUSINESS SALE, read one headline; EERIE LOTTERY A GREAT SUCCESS—WINNER GOES TO SPAIN, said another.

I was well into the December papers, looking at ads for big post-Christmas sales and reading weather reports predicting three more feet of snow when I found the picture of the boy: The boy from the photographs in the Stewarts' attic. There he was, in the lefthand corner of page one of the December 26th issue.

BOY, 11, DIES IN CHRISTMAS TRAGEDY, read the headline beneath his picture.

December 26

Rodney Stewart, age 11, was found dead in his bedroom on Christmas morning by his parents, Mr. and Mrs. James Stewart.

"It was just terrible," sobbed Mrs. Stewart as she sat surrounded by the pile of unopened Christmas presents bearing tags with little Rodney's name on them. "Christmas was his favorite time of year."

"We don't know why he expired so soon," said Mr. Stewart, stroking the dog he'd bought for his son's birthday only a few months ago. "Just the night before he'd seemed so fresh."

Mr. and Mrs. Stewart have been residents of Eerie for many years. Mr. Stewart owns the Two Left Feet dance studio. The cause of the boy's death is unknown. Chief Hoffa of the Eerie police department has, however, ruled out foul play.

That was it. Just a small article. No explanation of how Rodney died. I frantically thumbed through the rest of the papers, hoping there would be a follow-up article. But there was nothing. I turned back to the page and ripped the section out, putting it in my pocket with the other one.

Instead of getting clearer, things were getting more complicated. All I had to go on were parents who never seemed to age and a kid who had died on Christmas Eve in 1976. And hadn't Mrs. Stewart called Simon "Rodney" by mistake? Somehow Simon was involved in all of it, but why? The only way I was going to find out was by getting inside that house.

I left the library, waving good-bye to Mr. Poe, who was walking back and forth muttering something about a bird. I grabbed my bike and started to ride home. I needed to make some plans for getting into the Stewart house that night.

As I crossed the street, I made sure to check for oncoming cars. I was looking one way when I heard someone shout.

"Hey, look out!"

I stopped my bike just before I hit someone.

"Sorry," I said, looking up. "I wasn't paying . . ."

It was Mr. Stewart. He had just come out of World of Stuff, and his arms were loaded with bags. When he saw that it was me, he turned bright red.

"Marshall. Hello. I, um . . ."

"That's okay," I said nervously. I didn't know what to do. I felt the pictures of the Stewarts and their dead kid burning a hole in my shirt pocket.

"Just getting ready for a party," Mr. Stewart said, indicating the bags filled with hats and streamers and napkins.

"Oh, a party," I said.

"A birthday party. A belated birthday." He smiled. "Did you find your friend yet?"

I tried to stay calm. I didn't want him to know that I knew that Simon was being kept prisoner in his house.

"Not yet," I said. "I guess he must have had something to do. Come to think of it, I'm pretty sure I remember him saying he was going away for a few days."

Mr. Stewart nodded. "Oh, good. I mean, good that you're not worried about him. Good that you don't think he's . . . missing or anything."

"Nope, nothing like that," I said, trying to sound carefree. "Well, I better let you get back to your party."

"Oh, thanks. I wish I could invite you, but it's sort of a . . . a family thing. You know how it is."

"That's okay," I said. "Have a great time."

Mr. Stewart continued on across the street and got into his car. I started pedaling. By the time I reached the corner, I was going faster than I'd ever gone before, trying to get away from him.

I went home and stowed the two newspaper clippings in the Evidence Locker in the Secret Spot. Then I packed my spy bag with necessary equipment: flashlight, rope, screwdriver, gloves, mask, and a chocolate bar. Hey, you never know when you're going to get hungry waiting for aliens to appear, right? It was my parents' bowling night, and Syndi was staying over at a friend's house, so I left a note saying that Simon and I were camping out and left the house.

Once more I rode my bike to the Stewarts' house. This time I was careful to take back roads, so that no one would see me. I hid my bike in the trees and snuck around to the garage. Standing by the window, I shined the flashlight inside. Simon's bike was still there.

I looked up at the house. The downstairs windows were still black, but I could see light coming from somewhere on the second floor. I tried to remember how the house was laid out, and determined that the light was coming from where Mr. and Mrs. Stewart's bedroom was.

I walked over to the house and stood underneath the window, listening for any sounds. The air was warm, and the Stewarts had left their window open. I could hear them talking as they moved around.

"Everything is ready for the big day," Mrs. Stewart said. "This is going to be so exciting. He'll be so happy. Did you seal him in for the night?"

"Yes, dear," said Mr. Stewart.

"Did you remember to burp him? Don't forget what happened the last time." She sounded sad.

"Yes, dear," said Mr. Stewart again. "I was very careful."

"Good," said Mr. Stewart. "We want him to be as fresh as possible for his big day."

Burp him? What was she talking about? Simon wasn't a baby. Mrs. Stewart was talking nonsense.

She started to hum then, the same chirpy song I'd heard her humming when I was working for her. As she walked around the room getting ready for bed, the sound got louder and softer as she passed the window and then moved away from it. The tune filled my head, until pretty soon I was humming it, too.

Then she began to sing along:

Our goal has always been
To seal the freshness in
For-ev-er.

I knew I'd heard those words before. They were part of a song, a song I'd heard someone else singing.

Mrs. Stewart was talking again.

"All tucked in, dear?"

"Yes, honeybun."

"Okay, then. Hands inside and I'll seal us up."

The light went out. Then there was a soft whooshing sound, like the electric doors closing at the supermarket. This was followed by a soft *plup*.

Suddenly, I knew where I'd heard the song before. I knew where I'd heard the same whooshing sound before, and I knew why Mr. Stewart had to burp Simon. Worst of all, I knew why the Stewarts hadn't aged in over twenty years. My mind reeled as I thought back to something that Simon and I had encountered right after I first moved to Eerie. Something so strange, so weird, so bizarre that no one would ever believe it in a million years.

And now it was back again.

My ears rang with the sound of those words I'd heard. Over and over they played in my head, like a song on a radio. But no matter how hard I tried to turn the radio off, the song kept playing.

Foreverware, for wives and mothers everywhere.
Our goal has always been
To seal the freshness in
For-ev-er.

Foreverware, for any dish that you prepare.
For each and every meal
We have the perfect seal.
The muffins that you bake
Will still be fresh in early May,
The coffee cake, your cinnamon ring
Will last at least until next spring.

It works on almost everything!
Foreverware!

There was no doubt about it. Mrs. Stewart had been singing the Foreverware theme song. All of a sudden, it all came rushing back to me at once. The creepy identical twins. Their crazy mother. Everything.

You see, right after my family moved to Eerie, we got a visit from Mrs. Betty Wilson, one of our next-door neighbors. She brought over a sample of Foreverware, these plastic containers for keeping food in. She said that whatever you put in Foreverware would stay fresh forever. It seemed great, especially for someone like my mom, who isn't the neatest housekeeper in the world. She wanted my mom to buy a whole case of the stuff. Then later, at Mrs. Wilson's house, I'd heard a whole group of women singing the theme song—the one I'd heard Mrs. Stewart humming but didn't recognize until now.

Mrs. Wilson also brought along her twin boys, Bert and Ernie. I thought there was something strange about them. They dressed as though it was the 1960s, and they didn't say a word, even when I spoke to them. Then, when they left, one of them slipped me a note that said, "Yearbook, 1964." The next day, I checked out the B. F. Skinner Junior High 1964 yearbook, and there were Bert and Ernie, looking exactly the way they did when they were standing in my living room.

I knew something weird was happening. So that night, Simon and I snuck over to the Wilsons' house and climbed up a rose trellis outside the boys' bedroom window. We couldn't believe what we saw. There was Mrs. Wilson, and she was putting Bert and Ernie to bed—in gigantic plastic Foreverware containers. She was sealing them up inside as if they were leftovers or something, the way you'd put a sandwich in the refrigerator to keep it fresh. She even burped the beds, letting out the excess air the way you're supposed to by pressing on the center of the lid.

After she left, I climbed in and opened the beds to let Bert and Ernie out. That's when they told me that their mother had been keeping them in Foreverware ever since 1964, when their father had invented the product. They were really almost forty years old, but they still looked as though they were twelve. As long as they slept for eight hours a night in the Foreverware beds, they'd stay young forever.

But Bert and Ernie didn't want to be twelve forever. They wanted to grow up. They wanted to get out of the seventh grade and find out what it was like to be adults. That's why they'd asked me for help. When I let them out of the beds, it broke the Foreverware seal. That night they aged to where they really should be. Then they went in and opened their mother's Foreverware bed, and overnight she turned into the old woman she should have been all along.

The secret of Foreverware was my first introduction to Eerie's strangeness. It had started Simon's and my investigation. Just the thought of those creepy Foreverware beds made my skin grow cold. I thought that we'd seen the last of them when Bert and Ernie grew up. And I thought I'd heard the last of the Foreverware theme song when Mrs. Wilson had turned old. But now Mr. and Mrs. Stewart were up there, probably sleeping in their very own vacuum-sealed plastic dish, keeping themselves young forever. Since they looked just like they did in the newspaper photograph, I guessed they must have been doing it since at least 1976.

But that still didn't explain what had happened to their son and the other kids in the photographs, or what they wanted with Simon. And it didn't give me any ideas about how I was going to get him out of there.

It just made me realize that I had to do it soon.

I started to walk around the house, hoping that maybe one of the windows would be open and I could climb in. But they were all locked up tight. The Stewarts had been very careful to make sure that they kept everyone out of their house—or everyone in. Finally, I sat down on the back steps and tried to think of another plan.

That's when I noticed the dog door. Down at the bottom of the back door there was a hole cut into the wood. A hinged flap covered the opening, so that the dog could go in and out whenever he wanted to. It wasn't huge, but I figured I could squeeze through it. If it was open.

I pushed on the flap, and it moved. I lifted it up and peered inside, right into the Stewarts' kitchen. I'd found my way in.

"Here, Spike," I called softly. I wanted to make sure the dog wasn't around, so he wouldn't bark and alert the Stewarts.

When I didn't hear anything, I tried putting my head and shoulders through the door. It was a tight fit, but by putting my arms through first, I was able to squish my shoulders up and just make it through. There was a horrible moment when I thought I was stuck halfway, but I wiggled around until I got loose and was able to pull myself into the kitchen. The dog door closed behind me, and I was sitting in the darkness, my heart beating a mile a minute.

I stayed there for a few minutes, just listening to the sound of the refrigerator humming and the clock on the wall ticking. The clock cat's rhinestones glittered in the darkness, and its creepy eyes were wide open, as if it was watching me.

I listened for any sign that the Stewarts had woken up. When I was pretty sure that everything was clear, I crept over to the fridge and opened the door. Just as I had suspected, the shelves were lined with row after row of Foreverware containers. Thin sandwich boxes, tall pickle keepers, round bowls of fruit salad. Each one was carefully dated and labeled. I picked one up and looked at it. COLESLAW, JULY 1979, it said on the lid. I carefully opened it and looked inside. Sure enough, there was a mound of shredded cabbage, still as fresh as the day Mrs. Stewart had sealed it up. The mayonnaise glistened, the carrots were bright and crisp. I shuddered and put the lid back on.

Just looking at it all made me want to run screaming from the house. There was something unnatural about food that had lasted since before I was born.

I shut the refrigerator, switched on my flashlight, and started to walk through the house. I knew Simon had to be in there somewhere, but I didn't know where. As I passed from one dark, empty room to the next, I had to think hard to remember the layout of the house.

I walked down the first floor hallway, peering into each room as I passed by. In the living room, the mirrored ball was spinning slowly and silently in the darkness, the little panes of glass catching the beam from my flashlight and turning it into thousands of tiny twinkles. But Simon wasn't in there.

I passed by the dining room and the rec room, pausing briefly at each one but finding nothing. Then I came to the stairs leading up to the second floor. I didn't want to go up there, but I had to find Simon and help him. Taking a deep breath, I put one foot on the stair and started up. The step let out a sharp groan as I put my weight on it, and I stopped dead in my tracks, waiting for the sound of someone coming for me.

When nothing happened, I continued up the stairs, going as slowly as I could. Finally I reached the second floor. Not wanting my flashlight to give me away, I put my hand over the end so that only a thin beam of light could escape. It made it a little harder to see, but I had to take the risk of tripping over something in the dark. If the Stewarts saw the light, they'd catch me.

Again I went from room to room. The bathroom. The sewing room. Both empty. I paused at the door to Mr. and Mrs. Stewart's room. Luckily for me, it was closed. I went by it and kept moving down the hallway to the room Mrs. Stewart had kept locked.

There was something new on the door—a small sign with a picture of a baseball player swinging at a ball and the words RODNEY'S ROOM printed on it. The room must have belonged to the Stewarts' little boy before he died. Now they were using it again. Something told me that behind that door I would find my best friend.

I reached for the handle and turned. The knob slid a little ways and then stopped dead. It was still locked. I tried again, but no matter how hard I tried to turn the knob, it wouldn't budge. I was locked out.

"Simon?" I whispered softly. "Are you in there?"

There was no answer. I thought about trying to break the door down, or attempting to open the lock with the screwdriver in my backpack. But I knew both of those things would make too much noise. Even if I did get the door open and found Simon, it was sure to wake the Stewarts. Finding him wouldn't do either of us any good if we couldn't get out again.

I looked at the door handle again. If it was locked from the outside, then there had to be a key that would open it. And if there was a key, it was probably hidden somewhere safe—maybe in the Stewarts' bedroom. I was going to have to go in and find it.

Turning my flashlight off, I walked back to their bedroom door, feeling my way along the wall through the blackness. As I stood outside the door, my heart racing, I kept saying to myself, "You're doing this for Simon. You're doing this for Simon. You're doing this for Simon."

With my hand shaking, I reached out and turned the doorknob. It slid open with a slight scraping sound, and I pushed the door open a crack. Putting my eye to it, I looked inside. The Stewarts' window was still open, and the moonlight coming in was enough to see by.

In the center of the room was their big Foreverware bed. The top was pulled down and sealed shut, and the moonlight shone softly on the plastic lid. I tried not to look at it too much as I slipped into the room and started to search for the key.

I tried the dresser first, hoping that maybe the key was sitting there along with the bottles of perfume, tubes of lipstick, and dish of pennies. But it was nowhere to be found. I did find a key ring, but all it had on it was a set of car keys. I set it down and moved on.

The only other items of furniture in the room were the two bedside tables that sat on either side of the giant Foreverware container. I didn't want to go anywhere near that thing, but I didn't have a choice. I went to the closest one and looked down.

What I saw was Mrs. Stewart's face. She was lying there smiling, her eyes closed as she slept. Her lips were parted, and her breath made little clouds on the Foreverware lid. She had her hair in big rollers, and her face was covered in a film of blue cold cream. It was all I could do not to run out of the room.

I tried not to look at Mrs. Stewart as I searched her nightstand. It was crowded with things like tissues, a bottle of sleeping tablets, and an alarm clock, so it was hard to find anything. There were several books stacked there as well, including *How to Have An Ageless Body, The Guide to Eternal Youth,* and *Everlasting Goodness: The Foreverware Recipe Book.*

I'd almost given up on finding the key when I noticed the string hanging down from the knob of the lamp on the table. Something on the end sparkled in the moonlight and caught my eye as I was turning to go search Mr. Stewart's side of the bed. I reached out for it and saw that it was a key. I hoped that it was the one I needed.

Backing out of the bedroom, I closed the door again and walked back down the hall, the key pressed against my palm. When I got to Rodney's room, I put the key in the lock and turned it. When I felt the lock click open, I nearly shouted for joy. The hardest part was over.

Inside, the room was pitch black. I wanted to just flick the wall switch and turn on the light, but I was afraid the Stewarts would wake up. So I shut the door behind me and turned the flashlight on again, shining it around the room.

Rodney's bedroom looked like any other boy's room, except that everything was straight out of 1976. The walls were covered in red, white, and blue striped wallpaper, and there were posters of baseball players hanging everywhere—Reggie Jackson, Pete Rose—all the great players from back then. Model airplanes hung from the ceiling, and there was a hockey stick and a basketball in one corner.

On one side of the room was a set of Foreverware bunk beds. They looked just like the one in the Stewarts' bedroom, except that they were smaller. I walked over and looked through the lid of the bottom one. Inside, Simon was sleeping quietly.

I grabbed one corner of the bed's lid and pulled hard. There was a low hissing sound as it came free and the air inside escaped. I pushed the lid aside and looked at Simon. He was yawning and rubbing his eyes.

"Mars!" he said when he saw me looking down at him.

"Shhh," I said, putting my finger to my lips. "We don't want to wake them up."

"How'd you find me?" Simon asked, sitting up. He

was dressed in pajamas that had cowboys and horses all over them.

"It's a long story," I said. "I'll fill you in later. What happened to you?"

Simon scratched his head. "I showed up after school like I was supposed to," he said. "Mrs. Stewart was acting kind of weird. I mean, weirder than usual. She kept asking me these strange questions, like what kind of cake I liked and stuff like that. Then, when I told her that my parents had gone away for a week, she got all excited. I told her I wanted to get to work in the attic, and the next thing I knew she had put this sack over my head and I couldn't see anything."

"That must have been when I showed up," I said. "I heard a lot of noise in the house, but she wouldn't let me in."

"That was me crashing around," said Simon. "I tried to run, but I couldn't see anything. I kept tripping over stuff. I broke a lamp. Finally, I fell over the couch and blacked out. When I woke up, I was locked in here. You should have heard me scream when I saw the Foreverware bed."

"I know how you feel," I said. "When I finally realized what that song was she was humming, I thought my heart would stop."

"What are they doing?" asked Simon.

"This is Rodney's room," I said. "You know, the

kid from the picture. Their son. I found out he died in 1976.''

"Mrs. Stewart kept calling me 'Rodney,' " Simon said. "It was like she thought I was him or something. She kept saying how nice it was that the family was back together again. I didn't know what she meant."

"I think she's nuts," I said. "I think both of them are nuts. Nothing in this house has changed since 1976, the year Rodney died."

"How did he die, and what do they want with me?" asked Simon.

"I don't know how he died. But I think they want you to be their new kid," I said.

Simon's eyes went wide. "You've got to be joking."

I shook my head. "I told you—they're insane. We have to get out of here fast. Where are your clothes?"

"I don't know. Mrs. Stewart made me wear this old stuff of Rodney's."

"You'll have to wear those pajamas then. Let's go."

I opened the bedroom door and looked into the hall. Everything was clear.

"Come on," I whispered to Simon. "And be quiet."

I crept down the hall, moving extra slowly when we reached the Stewarts' bedroom. Then I went down the stairs, motioning to Simon to avoid the creaky step at the bottom. We were in the downstairs hall before I could even breathe freely again. We were almost home free.

"Okay," I said quietly. "Now all we have to do is go out the back door."

Simon nodded, and followed me to the kitchen. I could see the door. Only a few feet separated us from freedom. I started to move more quickly.

All of a sudden, the kitchen light snapped on, stopping me dead in my tracks.

"Going somewhere?" asked a voice.

9

*M*rs. Stewart was sitting at the kitchen table, look-ing at us and frowning. She had on a pink bath-robe, and her face was still smeared with the blue cream, so that she looked like some kind of freaky alien in curlers. She was tapping her long red nails against the tabletop, and the clicking sound filled the air. A piece of cheesecake sat on a plate in front of her.

"I guess it's a good thing I came down for a little midnight snack," she said. Then she looked right at Simon. "Rodney, I thought I told you—no overnight visitors without permission."

"His name isn't Rodney," I said. "It's Simon. You're crazy, and we're leaving."

Mrs. Stewart jumped up. "Not so fast!" she shrieked. She was standing between us and the back door, blocking our exit.

"Quick!" I said to Simon. "Head for the front door."

We turned around to make our escape and ran smack into Mr. Stewart, who was standing right behind us. His arms went around us, and we couldn't break free.

"Let us go!" I yelled as I tried to pull away from his grip.

Mrs. Stewart came over and took Simon by the arm. Mr. Stewart continued to hold me tightly.

"Rodney," said Mrs. Stewart. "I'm very disappointed that you've disobeyed me. Especially after all the trouble your father and I went through for your birthday party tomorrow."

"Birthday?" said Simon. "Tomorrow's not my birthday. My birthday isn't until October. What are you talking about?" He was struggling, trying to wrench his arm out of her grasp.

"You listen to your mother," Mr. Stewart said to Simon. "She knows best."

"She's not my mother," Simon shouted. "And you're not my father. My name is Simon. Simon Holmes."

Mrs. Stewart started to cry, making the face cream run down her cheeks in blue rivers. "Rodney," she said. "Don't you want to make Mommy happy?"

"No!" yelled Simon. "I want to go home. Now let me go."

"I know," said Mr. Stewart. "How about if we let

your friend here stay the night. Would that make you feel better?''

Simon looked at me. It was obvious that the Stewarts were crazy. For whatever strange reasons, they wanted to pretend that Simon was their dead kid. I knew they wouldn't just let us go. Our only choice was to try and play along and look for a chance to escape as soon as we could. I nodded at Simon.

"Okay," he said uncertainly. "I'd like that."

Mrs. Stewart stopped crying and smiled. "Good," she said sweetly. "That's my boy. Let's get you two upstairs and into bed before it's too late. It's already way past your bedtime, and you know what happens if you don't get enough sleep. Then tomorrow we'll have a great big party. You'd like that, wouldn't you?''

Simon smiled weakly at her. "That would be great," he said.

The Stewarts marched us back up the stairs and into Rodney's room. Just looking at the Foreverware bunk beds made my stomach knot up, but I knew there was no other way. I watched as Simon got into the lower bed and Mrs. Stewart tucked him in.

"Sleep tight," she said as she pulled the lid over him. "Don't let the bedbugs bite." There was a hissing sound as she pressed the lid down securely and then lifted one corner to let the excess air out.

"Now it's your turn," she said to me. "Up you go."

I climbed up the ladder and got into the top bunk. Mr. and Mrs. Stewart lifted the Foreverware lid and placed it over me. Then I heard the same familiar hissing as they shut me in for the night. A few seconds later, the lights went out as they left the room. I lay there in the bed, feeling like a piece of leftover chicken. I'd never wanted to get out of anyplace more than I wanted to get out of that bed. It felt like a coffin.

As soon as I was sure the Stewarts were back in their own bed, I reached under my shirt. When Mr. Stewart had grabbed me, I'd managed to keep hold of my backpack. When they weren't looking, I'd hidden it under my shirt. Somehow, in all the excitement they hadn't noticed.

I unzipped the pack and felt around for the screwdriver. When I had it, I pushed the end into the groove where the bed's lid was pressed against the rim. It just fit into the crack. Then I pulled down on the screwdriver, forcing the lid up. I moved the screwdriver over a few inches and did it again. Each time, the lid moved up a little bit more. Finally, I pushed up on the plastic surface and felt the whole thing pop up.

Sitting up, I shoved the lid aside and crawled out of the bed. I climbed down the ladder and quickly opened up Simon's bed.

"Thanks," he said. "*Now* are we getting out of here?"

I shook my head. "They've probably locked us in," I said. I went to the door and tried the knob. Sure enough, it was stuck fast, and it was locked from the outside.

"So what do we do?" asked Simon.

"We wait until tomorrow," I said. "Mrs. Stewart said something about throwing you . . . I mean Rodney . . . a birthday party. If we play along, maybe we'll be able to figure out how to get out of here."

"I wish someone knew we were missing," Simon said. "My parents won't be back for a week."

"And I told mine we were camping out so we could watch for UFOs," I said. "They won't even miss us until tomorrow night."

"I wish we knew what happened to the real Rodney," said Simon. "I mean how he died. That might help."

"All I know is that he was found on Christmas morning," I said. "The paper didn't say anything else."

Simon sighed. "I'm not sitting around here until Christmas Eve," he said. "I guess all we can do is wait until tomorrow and see what happens."

"I'd better put you back in that thing," I said, nodding at the bed. "We don't want them to know we got out."

Simon shuddered. "Now I know how Bert and Ernie felt," he said. "No wonder they wanted to grow up."

Simon got back into bed and I put the lid back over

him. Then I put the lid over my bed and pushed down, sealing three of the corners. I squeezed under the third one and tried to pull the edge down as far as possible. It still wasn't sealed completely, and I hoped the Stewarts wouldn't notice when they came in the next morning.

I shut my eyes and tried to go to sleep. But my mind was filled with the image of Rodney in the photograph, smiling and laughing as the puppy licked his face. I tried to imagine him sleeping every night in the Foreverware bed, sealed up by his mother. I wondered what exactly had happened to him on that Christmas Eve in 1976. Whatever it was, I knew it held the clue to our escape.

Eventually, I must have drifted off, because the next thing I knew, Mrs. Stewart was pulling the lid off of my bed. I saw it slide back, and then her smiling face was looking down at me.

"Good morning," she said cheerfully, as though it was perfectly normal to kidnap two kids and keep them locked up in giant plastic kitchenware. "How did you sleep?"

"Fine," I lied.

"I see your lid was a little loose this morning," she said.

"I must have been tossing in my sleep," I said. "I do that sometimes."

"You have to be careful about things like that," she

said. "That's how spoilage occurs, you know. That's how Rodney. . . ."

All of a sudden, she stopped, as though she was remembering something horrible.

"That's how Rodney what?" I asked, prodding her.

"Nothing," she said. "Rodney is just fine. In fact, today's his big day, isn't it? Now let's get downstairs and get started."

She'd already opened Simon's bed, and he was standing in front of the dresser, looking at himself in the mirror. He was dressed in a pair of blue and white striped shorts and a red shirt. Something about the outfit looked familiar. Then I realized why. It was the same outfit that Rodney had been wearing in the photograph of his birthday party we'd found in the attic.

"I feel stupid," said Simon. "I look like a flag or something. Why can't I wear my own clothes?"

Mrs. Stewart patted him on the shoulder. "But those are your clothes. They're your favorites. remember? I thought you'd want to wear them on your birthday."

"I keep telling you," Simon said. "It's *not* my birthday. And I have to get to school."

Mrs. Stewart laughed. "Don't be silly. You don't need to attend school," she said. She paused for a few seconds. "You're eleven today. Of course, thanks to the miracle of Foreverware, you're *always* eleven, aren't you? I don't know what we'd do without it."

Simon was looking at me in the mirror. "What now?" he mouthed silently.

I shook my head. "Just play along," I mouthed back.

"Why don't we go downstairs for your birthday breakfast?" Mrs. Stewart said. "I think your father has prepared your favorite."

"What would that be?" asked Simon.

Mrs. Stewart laughed again. "Oh, you're such a kidder," she said. "Now go on, get downstairs, the both of you."

Simon and I went downstairs, followed closely by Mrs. Stewart, who was careful never to let us get too far away from her. As we walked into the kitchen, the smell of something cooking filled the air. Mr. Stewart was standing at the stove, busily flipping pancakes over on a sizzling griddle.

"Well, if it isn't the birthday boy!" he said when we appeared. "And how are we today?"

"Fine," said Simon.

Mr. Stewart grinned. "Good," he said. "All ready for some of Dad's famous flapjacks?"

"I guess so," said Simon, not sounding happy about it at all.

Mr. Stewart brought over a steaming pile of pancakes and set it down on the table. He had made the pancakes so that each one was shaped like a different animal. He dropped what looked like a pig onto my plate.

"And for you," he said as he gave Simon his, "an elephant. Your favorite."

Sure enough, Simon's pancake had two big ears and a long, thin trunk. It sat in the middle of Simon's plate as Mrs. Stewart put a glob of butter on it and then poured a stream of sticky syrup across it.

"Doesn't that look yummy?" she said.

Simon picked up his fork and cut off a piece of the elephant's ear. He raised the fork to his mouth and took a bite. He chewed slowly, tasting it. Then he actually smiled.

"Hey!" he said. "This is good."

Mr. Stewart grinned. "I thought you'd like it. I put something extra special in them just for you. Bananas."

Simon took another bite. Then another. If there's one way to make Simon forget that he's in trouble, it's to feed him. Pretty soon he was gobbling down pancakes so quickly you'd never know he was being held captive by some crazy people who thought he was their son.

"You're really eating a lot, *Rodney*," I said, trying to get Simon's attention.

He glanced up from eating the banana horse Mr. Stewart had just made for him, his fork raised halfway to his lips. He looked at the piece of pancake and then put it down again.

"I guess I'm full," he said to Mrs. Stewart.

She clapped her hands together. "Well, then," she said. "Maybe we should play some games."

"Games?" said Simon.

"Oh, yes," said Mrs. Stewart. "We have a whole day of fun planned for you. And this afternoon we'll have cake and a big surprise."

"Great," said Simon. "I can't wait."

While Mr. Stewart did the dishes, Mrs. Stewart herded us into the rec room and told us to sit down on the couch. Then she opened a closet and brought out a stack of boxes. She put them on the table and opened the top one.

"Let the fun begin!" she said.

For the rest of the morning, we played game after game. Mrs. Stewart was always in charge, shouting out orders or urging us on as we pinned the tail on the donkey, moved our pieces around the Monopoly game board, and tried to drop clothespins into the mouth of an old glass milk bottle. She made us play every horrible birthday party game in the book, and the whole time, she was laughing and smiling like a demented clown.

Finally, Mr. Stewart came into the room. "Okay," he said. "Time for the big party. Everyone into the kitchen."

We all trooped into the kitchen behind Mr. Stewart. While we'd been playing games, he'd been decorating. The whole room was filled with red, white, and blue balloons. Streamers hung from the ceiling. The table was covered with presents. And right in the middle of it all was a big cake. It was covered in white frosting, and in blue icing it said, "Happy Birthday, Rodney."

"Sit down. Sit down," said Mr. Stewart.

We all sat, and he put birthday hats on our heads, snapping the rubber bands under our chins. Then he handed Simon a present.

"Open this first," he said.

Simon looked doubtfully at the package in his hands.

"Go on," said Mrs. Stewart. "I think you'll like it."

Simon slowly peeled off the paper, exposing a box. He took the top off and lifted out a yo-yo. It was bright yellow.

"It glows in the dark," said Mrs. Stewart. "Isn't that groovy?"

"Really groovy," said Simon.

Mr. Stewart kept handing Simon gifts to open. Before long, he had a pile of toys that any kid would have envied—any kid alive in 1976.

When everything was opened, Mrs. Stewart poured glasses of punch, and Mr. Stewart lit the candles on the birthday cake.

"Okay," said Mr. Stewart. "Let's sing."

"Happy birthday to you . . ." began Mrs. Stewart. "Happy birthday to you . . ."

Sitting behind the cake, Simon looked miserable.

"Happy birthday dear Rodney . . ." warbled the Stewarts. "Happy birthday to you!"

"Blow out the candles," said Mr. Stewart. "And don't forget to make a wish."

Simon took a deep breath and blew. The candles all went out, little streams of smoke lifting up from the burned-out wicks. The Stewarts applauded.

"I bet I know what you wished for," said Mr. Stewart. He ran out of the room. I had no idea what he was up to.

Mr. Stewart returned carrying a big box with a giant bow on top. He set it on the floor beside Simon.

"Open it," he said.

Simon ripped the bow off the box and took off the lid. Inside was a big plastic container. A Foreverware container.

"What is it?" asked Simon. He sounded scared.

"Go on," urged Mrs. Stewart. "You'll see."

Simon lifted off the Foreverware lid, and a little cloud of frosty air escaped. Then there was a bark and Spike popped out. He looked up, his tail wagging, and licked Simon's face. At that very moment there was a flash, as Mrs. Stewart took a picture.

"It's Spike," Simon said.

"That's right," Mr. Stewart said. "He's been waiting a long time to see you again."

"You have Foreverware to thank for that," added

Mrs. Stewart. She was watching the camera spit out the picture she'd just taken. "And thanks to the magic of Polaroid, you can see the moment over and over."

She handed Simon the photograph. When he looked at it, his face went white. He handed the picture to me. It looked exactly like all of the birthday pictures we'd seen in the photo album. There was the dog and the box. There was the cat clock in the background. Only this time it was Simon's face in the middle.

I looked at Spike, who had hopped out of the box and was running around the kitchen. When I'd first seen him in the Stewarts' living room, I'd assumed he just *looked* like the dog from the photograph. Now I realized he *was* the dog from the photo. The Stewarts must have had him in Foreverware all this time.

We were looking at a twenty-one-year-old dog.

10

I could tell by the look on his face that Simon was realizing the same thing I had about Spike. His skin had turned from white to a funny shade of green, and he looked as if he was going to pass out.

"Let's have cake," said Mr. Stewart. He got a knife and cut a huge piece for each of us. When he set my plate in front of me, I couldn't help wondering if the cake was left over from twenty-one years ago, too. I took a bite and put it in my mouth. It tasted like plain old chocolate.

"How's the cake?" asked Mr. Stewart.

"Delicious," I said, because it really was, twenty years old or not.

Mrs. Stewart beamed. "I'm glad you like it. And if you like that, then you'll really like what we have planned for tomorrow."

"What's tomorrow?" Simon asked. "Not another birthday party."

"Oh, no," said Mrs. Stewart. "Something even better."

She looked at Mr. Stewart, who nodded. "Well, we were going to surprise you," Mrs. Stewart continued, "but I guess we'll tell you now. We're going to celebrate Christmas."

"Christmas?" Simon and I said together.

Mrs. Stewart smiled. "Well, I know it's early, but I know how much Rodney loves Christmas," she said. "And after last time, well . . ."

"What happened last time?" I asked. I was hoping she'd talk about what happened the Christmas that Rodney—the real Rodney—died.

Mrs. Stewart started to sniffle. "That's all in the past now," she said. "What's important is that we're a family again. Now we can have a *real* Christmas."

Mr. Stewart put his arm around Mrs. Stewart, who was still sniffling a little bit. "It's all right, Martha," he said. "Everything will be fine."

Then he turned to Simon and me. "Why don't we do something fun to cheer Mother up?"

"Why don't we go to a movie?" suggested Simon. I knew he was trying to find a way to get us out of there.

Mr. Stewart frowned. "Now, you know we can't go out of the house, young man," he said. "Now that your mother and I have you back, we want to keep you all to ourselves. Same with your friend there. But that should be okay with you, right? You always said you wanted a brother. Now you have one. We'll be one cozy little family. Think of it as our most special Christmas present ever.''

I tried to imagine spending an eternity with the Stewarts. It was clear that they intended to keep us in the house forever. With the help of Foreverware, we'd just keep living the same days over and over and over. I pictured Simon opening the box with Spike in it year after year. I saw myself eating plate after plate of animal-shaped pancakes. I couldn't let that happen. I needed a plan.

''I know,'' I said, getting an idea. ''Why don't we play hide-and-seek. That's one of your *favorite* games, isn't it, Rodney?''

I kicked Simon under the table. ''Ow. I mean, yeah, I really love that game.''

''I don't know,'' said Mrs. Stewart. I could tell she wasn't very happy about the idea of us leaving her sight.

Simon looked at her, his eyes wide. ''Please,'' Simon said sadly. ''Mom.''

At the sound of the word ''mom,'' Mrs. Stewart looked as if she were going to cry.

''Oh, okay,'' she said. ''It might be fun after all. And if my little boy wants to play, well then, I guess we will. Who will be It?''

"Dad has to be It," Simon said. "And we'll all hide."

Mr. Stewart closed his eyes and started to count. "One, Two, Three . . ."

Simon, Mrs. Stewart, and I left the room.

"I'll hide in the sewing room," Mrs. Stewart whispered to us. "He'll never think to look in there."

"Good idea," I said. "We'll hide somewhere else."

As soon as Mrs. Stewart was gone, I grabbed Simon and pulled him into the bathroom, shutting the door behind us.

"Okay," I said. "Here's the deal. I'm going to go get help. You have to stay here."

"Oh, no," Simon said. "You're not leaving me here alone again."

"It's the only way," I told him. "If we both leave, they'll come looking for us. But if I'm the only one gone, you can just say I'm hiding somewhere really good."

Simon groaned. "Okay," he said. "But hurry. I don't know how much longer I can keep this up."

We left the bathroom. In the kitchen, Mr. Stewart was still counting. ". . . Forty-two, Forty-three, Forty-four . . ."

"I'll hide in the living room," I told Simon. "When he goes looking for you, I'll sneak out."

Simon nodded. Then he walked upstairs, making sure

he made enough noise that Mr. Stewart was sure to hear him and know where he was. I went into the living room and crouched behind the sofa.

". . . Ninety-eight, Ninety-nine, One hundred," said Mr. Stewart. "Ready or not, here I come."

He came out of the kitchen and into the hallway. I could see his shadow on the wall as he looked around, deciding which way to go. I saw him move toward the living room, and I flattened myself against the floor as he appeared in the doorway.

"I wonder if anyone is in here?" he said.

I could feel my heart beating crazily in my chest as I held my breath. If Mr. Stewart caught me, it would all be over. I only had one chance. He took a few steps into the room, looking around. If he came too close, he would see me behind the couch.

Then he turned and left again. I let out a sigh of relief and risked looking over the edge of the couch. He was gone. I listened to him walking down the hallway, opening doors and looking into all the rooms.

When I heard him go up the stairs, I ran into the kitchen. Getting on my hands and knees, I stuck my head through the dog door for the second time and pulled myself through. As I crawled out Spike's dog door, I knew what I had to do. I had to find the only people who could help me now. I had to find Bert and Ernie.

I ran as fast as I could across the lawn toward the garage. I was sure that the Stewarts must have heard me crawling through Spike's door, and would be on my trail in no time. But when I reached the garage and finally looked behind me, there was no sign of them anywhere. Still, I didn't have a lot of time. Eventually they would notice I was gone.

Moving faster than I ever thought I could, I dashed for the trees. Luckily, no one had found my bike. I hopped on and sped down the street, my legs working overtime as I pushed the bike harder and harder.

After Simon and I had freed the Wilson twins from their Foreverware nightmare and they'd grown up to their rightful age, they'd become seventh-grade teachers at B. F. Skinner Junior High. They figured that they'd been through the same grade for so many years that they might as well put what they'd learned to good use. Now Ernie taught English, and Bert taught algebra. Or maybe it was the other way around. I was never sure which twin was which. They both worked in the mornings and left school together after lunch.

They'd sold the house they'd grown up in and moved to another one in a different part of town. Still, I knew where it was, and it didn't take me long to find their street and then their house: 1313 Twin Peaks Lane. Leaving my bike in the grass, I ran up to the door and pounded as hard as I could. My lungs were burning from riding so fast, and I thought I might pass out.

After what seemed like an eternity, the front door opened and one of the twins appeared.

"Marshall?" he said. "What are you doing here? Shouldn't you be in school?"

"I . . . need . . . your . . . help," I gasped.

"Are you doing poorly in algebra again?" the twin asked, making me think it was probably Bert. I'd had him the year before for that class, and I hadn't done too well.

"No," I said. "It's even worse than that."

"Worse than algebra?" said Ernie, appearing at his brother's side. "What's worse than that?"

"Don't mind him," said Bert. "He never was good with numbers."

"Look," I said. "This isn't about school. It's about Simon. He's been kidnapped."

"Kidnapped?" the twins said in unison. "By who?" asked Bert.

"You mean by *whom*," said Ernie.

"By Mr. and Mrs. Stewart," I said.

The twins' faces went white. "You mean Martha Stewart?" they said together. "James and Martha Stewart?"

I nodded. "They caught me, too, but I got out. You

have to help me get Simon away from them. They're keeping him in Forever . . .''

"Shhh," the twins said, holding their fingers to their lips. "Don't say that too loud. Come inside."

I went inside, and they shut the door. Bert led me into the living room, where I sat down on the couch. Bert and Ernie sat down on matching chairs.

"Martha Stewart," said Ernie, shaking his head.

"We used to play with her son, little Rod Stewart," added Bert.

"That's him," I said. I explained about how Simon and I had found Rodney's picture in the attic, and about how Mr. and Mrs. Stewart were pretending that Simon was Rodney now. "It's too weird," I said. "Why are they doing this?"

Bert sighed. "It's a sad story," he said. "Martha Stewart used to be one of the top Foreverware salespeople around. Only Mother had a better record than she did. They were great rivals, always trying to outdo each other."

"Then one year the Stewarts discovered that Rodney had a heart condition," Ernie said, taking up the story. "After that, the Stewarts were very overprotective. Especially Mrs. Stewart. She hardly ever let him outside to play, and she made him sleep in the Foreverware for even longer than usual. She thought it would make his heart stronger."

"But it didn't," said Bert. "In fact, it made it worse, because Rodney wasn't growing at all. We started seeing him less and less. Then, at Christmastime in 1976, he died."

"But how did he die?" I asked. "And why is Mrs. Stewart so obsessed with Christmas? She's planning on celebrating it tomorrow."

Ernie looked at Bert, and they both nodded. "Well," said Ernie, "that Christmas Eve, she put Rodney to bed. He was so excited. Christmas was his favorite time of the year. And every year he said he wanted to stay up and see Santa Claus come down the chimney. But of course Mrs. Stewart would never let him, because he had to stay sealed up in his bed."

"But in 1976, he *did* stay up," said Bert. "When Mrs. Stewart put him to bed for the night, she forgot to completely burp his container. There was still a little air left inside. Later that night, Rodney thought he heard Santa's sleigh and the reindeer on the roof. He was so excited that he pushed on the lid of his bed and . . ."

"It came off," finished Ernie.

They both looked at me, not saying anything.

"And he died," I said.

"We prefer to say he passed his expiration date," the twins said.

"Mrs. Stewart had a breakdown," said Bert. "She

was convinced that she was responsible for Rodney's expiration.''

"Ever since then, she's kept the house exactly as it was in 1976,'' said Ernie.

"We had no idea she'd do something like this,'' they chimed together.

"Okay,'' I said. "So she's trying to re-create Christmas of 1976, using Simon as Rodney. How do we get him out of there?''

Bert and Ernie whispered together for a minute. Then they turned to me.

"We have a plan,'' they said.

11

"Oh, no," I said. "I am *not* going back in that house."

The twins had just told me their plan, and I wasn't happy about it at all. They wanted me to go back to the Stewarts'.

"You have to, Marshall," said Bert. "If they think you've gone for help, there's no telling what they'll do. As long as you're out, Simon is in danger."

I sighed. "Okay," I said. "I'll go back. But this had better work, or we're all in trouble."

"Don't worry," the twins said. "It will work. We're sure of it."

Bert and Ernie walked me to the door. I got back on my bike and started off as they waved good-bye from the front steps. As I made my way back to the creepy house, I hoped they knew what they were doing.

When I reached the house, I checked my watch. I'd been gone for almost an hour, more than enough time for the Stewarts to notice I was missing. I expected them to be searching everywhere for me.

But when I stuck my head through the dog door, the house was quiet. The kitchen was empty, and there was no sign of the Stewarts or Simon. I crawled inside and went into the living room. It was empty, too. I couldn't figure out where everyone was.

Then I heard the sounds of people running overhead, followed by giggling and laughing. All of a sudden, there were footsteps on the stairs, and the Stewarts rushed down the hall and into the living room.

"Marshall!" said Mr. Stewart. "There you are. I've been looking all over the house for you. Simon said you were a good hider, but this is amazing. Where were you?"

I thought hard. "Um, I was . . ." I looked around, trying desperately to think of someplace I could have been hiding for an hour without being found. "I was . . ."

"In the attic," said Simon, coming into the room. "He was hiding in the attic."

"Yeah," I said. "That's right. I was up in the attic. Pretty smart, huh?"

"I'll say," said Mr. Stewart. "I even looked up there. Where were you?"

I looked at Simon. "Um . . . I was in a box," I said. It was the only thing I could think of.

"A *big* box," added Simon.

The Stewarts seemed to believe our story. Mrs. Stewart started to sit down.

"Where's Spike?" she asked. "He was here when we started to play."

"I don't know," said Mr. Stewart. "I haven't seen him."

She looked around the room, then went into the kitchen. A few seconds later, she came storming into the living room. She looked angry.

"He went out the dog door," she said. "It's wide open. And he's not the only one who's been coming and going."

"What do you mean?" said Mr. Stewart.

"There are dirty footprints on my nice clean linoleum," she said.

I looked down at my feet. My sneakers were covered with mud. In my rush to get inside, I hadn't even noticed it. There was a trail of dirty footprints leading from the kitchen and across the living room.

"Oh, no," I groaned. I'd been caught.

Mr. Stewart turned to Simon and me. "You boys get upstairs," he said angrily. "This game is over."

Simon and I started toward the stairs, but Mrs. Stewart stood in our way.

"No," she said. "Rodney may go to his room. But this one can't be trusted."

She grabbed me by the arm, her nails digging into my skin. "I'm going to make sure he doesn't cause any more trouble."

"Let me go!" I yelled.

Simon ran over and began pulling on my other arm, struggling with Mrs. Stewart. I felt like a wishbone about to be split in two.

"Leave him alone," said Simon. "He didn't do anything."

Mr. Stewart picked Simon up and started to carry him upstairs.

Simon was yelling the whole time, but there was nothing he could do.

"Now you," said Mrs. Stewart. "You come with me."

"Please," I said. "I want to stay with Simon—I mean Rodney."

"Oh, no," she said. "I can see what you're trying to do. You're trying to take him away from me. Well, I won't let that happen. Not again."

She dragged me into the kitchen and opened the door that led down to the cellar. In all my time in the house, I'd never been down there, and I didn't want to go now. I just knew there was something awful down there, something even worse than the Foreverware beds or Spike jumping out of that box again and again.

Pushing me in front of her, Mrs. Stewart made me

go down the cellar stairs. It was dark, and I almost stumbled several times as I made my way into the damp basement. The air was cool and wet, and I shivered as I imagined what might be down there.

When we reached the bottom of the stairs, Mrs. Stewart reached up and pulled a string, turning on a bare light bulb. The glow from it was weak, only enough to light a small circle in the basement, but when I looked down I could see things scurrying away into the darkness.

"Please," I said. "Don't leave me down here. I promise I won't try to run away."

Mrs. Stewart laughed. "Oh, you won't run away again," she said. "You're just like all the others. Well, I took care of them, and I'll take care of you, too."

She shoved me across the room, where she turned on another light bulb. This time, I could see what looked like a row of tall boxes lining one wall of the cellar. They were lined up neatly, one right beside the next.

"What are you doing?" I asked. "What are those?"

Mrs. Stewart walked me over to the boxes. As we got nearer, I realized that they were tall Foreverware containers. Mrs. Stewart went up to the first one and wiped her hand across the lid, cutting a path through the moisture that covered it. As the plastic cleared, I saw that behind it there was the face of a boy. At first I thought he was just sleeping. But then I saw that he seemed to be almost frozen. His skin was a pale color, and his eyes were closed. Below his face was a label affixed to the container: FREEZE DATE SEPTEMBER, 1978.

"Who is that?" I said. "What have you done to him?"

"It doesn't matter who he is," said Mrs. Stewart. She went to the next box and wiped that one. Another face appeared, and another label: FREEZE DATE FEBRUARY, 1982. She continued down the line, revealing box after box, each with a boy inside. There were six in all. The last box she came to was empty.

"All of these boys were like you," she said. "Bad boys who wouldn't do what they were told. All of them tried to ruin my Christmas celebration, just like you did. And all of them paid, just like you will."

That's when I realized who the boys were. They were the ones from the photographs. Mrs. Stewart had kidnapped all of them and forced them to act out Rodney's birthday. Then she had frozen them. I looked at the row of pale faces and started to scream.

She pushed me into the empty box.

"This is a very special Foreverware product," she said. "From the line of freezer accessories. Whatever is placed inside will stay fresh-frozen forever without being opened."

"You can't do this!" I shouted. "No!"

"I can't let you ruin Christmas," she said as she

placed the top over the container and began to press the sides closed. "I'm sure you understand."

As the lid sealed, I felt the air around me grow colder. My teeth began to chatter, and the box filled up with frosty mist. I pushed against the lid, but it didn't budge. I tried to scream, but it came out as a cloud. Through the lid, I saw the light in the cellar go out, and I knew Mrs. Stewart had left me alone, trapped for eternity in the Foreverware container.

After she left, I spent a long time banging on the lid of the Foreverware box, trying to push it open. But she had sealed it well, and it wasn't budging. After an hour of pounding, I hadn't gotten anywhere.

Even worse, I was starting to get sleepy. The air inside the box was cold, and it made me want to just close my eyes and drift off. But I knew that if I did, I would never wake up. I'd be trapped in the Stewart's basement like a pork chop waiting in a freezer for someone to thaw it out for dinner. Most likely, no one would ever find me, and I'd sit there with the other frozen boys forever.

I hopped up and down, trying to stay awake. The box was narrow, and there wasn't a lot of room, but I was able to move enough to keep myself conscious. Still, I couldn't keep it up forever. It was only a matter of time before I went to sleep for good.

Feeling my eyes start to close, I leaned against the

side of the box. The box shifted a little. Because I was on the end, there was nothing against that side of the container holding it up. I pulled back and leaned again. The box tilted a little bit more. That gave me an idea.

I threw myself against the side of the box, and it swayed. I did it again, harder, and it rocked even more. Shaking my head to stay awake, I began to pitch myself back and forth against the sides of the container, until it was moving with me. But my strength was fading fast, and even as I hurled myself at the sides I could feel myself losing consciousness. It was as though someone had turned out the light in my mind, and I was falling into frozen blackness.

Just before I passed out, I gave one more push against the wall. The container lurched sideways and leaned over, balancing on its edge. The last thing I remember feeling was the whole thing tumbling over like a tree falling down. Then everything went dark.

When I woke up, I was sprawled on the cellar floor. The container had tipped over, and the lid had popped free. I'd fallen out. Thankfully, I hadn't been hurt at all. I was still a little cold, and my head hurt, but at least I was alive.

Then I remembered the twins and their plan. I looked at my watch. It had broken when I fell, and I had no idea what time it was or how long I'd been lying there.

I didn't know how much time I had left before the rescue attempt began.

I stood up and dusted myself off. Then I turned and looked at the row of boxes that were still standing. I thought about letting all the other boys out, but I knew it would be too dangerous. If the Stewarts heard us, we'd all be done for.

"I promise I'll be back for you," I said as I went up the stairs.

12

At the cellar door, I tried looking through the key-hole. All I could see was a light coming from the other side. I heard voices, so I knew that the Stewarts were up to something.

"He'll be so surprised," Mrs. Stewart was saying. "This will be absolutely perfect."

"I hope he likes it," said Mr. Stewart. "I'd hate to be disappointed again. We've tried so many times."

"This one will be it," said Mrs. Stewart. "I just know it."

I turned the door knob and pushed it open. I slipped through the door and shut it behind me. From the kitchen, I could see Mr. and Mrs. Stewart moving around in the living room, but I couldn't see what they were doing. If I was quick, I could get out of the kitchen and up the stairs to Simon's room without being caught.

I moved silently into the hall. As I walked past the living room, I saw that the Stewarts were setting up a

Christmas tree. Actually, they were pulling it out of a giant Foreverware box. They must have saved it from the year Rodney died.

"Look," said Mrs. Stewart. "It's just as fresh as the day we first brought it back from the lot. Just smell that pine scent."

I hid behind the wall and peeked in, watching them as they set the tree up in one corner. Mr. Stewart kept moving the stand around, trying to find the perfect angle.

"That's fine, James," said Mrs. Stewart. "Now go get Rodney, and we can start decorating it. I'll get the eggnog."

Mr. Stewart started coming toward me. I had to act quickly. Dashing down the hall, I managed to sneak up the stairs before he saw me. I flew up to Rodney's room and opened the door. Simon was sitting on the bed.

"What happened to you?" he asked. "How are we getting out?"

"There's no time to explain," I said. "Mr. Stewart is coming. You have to play along with them. What time is it?"

"Ten o'clock," Simon said. "Why?"

I'd been knocked out on the cellar floor for longer than I thought. "That gives us about an hour," I said.

"An hour until what?" Simon asked.

I heard footsteps in the hallway as Mr. Stewart approached.

"Never mind," I said. "When it's time, you'll know."

Quickly I opened the door to the closet and slipped inside. I shut it just as Mr. Stewart opened the door.

"What was all that noise?" he said.

"Oh, nothing," said Simon. "I was just talking to myself."

"Well," said Mr. Stewart. "Come downstairs. Your mother and I have a big surprise for you."

I heard Simon and Mr. Stewart leave. A minute later, I opened the closet and went out into the hall. I snuck down the stairs and listened to the voices in the living room. When I was sure that all three of them were in there, I crept down the hallway and slipped into the coat closet. By leaving the door open a crack, I could see everything that was happening in the living room.

Simon was sitting on the couch. Mrs. Stewart was handing him a cup of eggnog, and Mr. Stewart was putting a record on the record player. A second later, music filled the room.

"Oh, I just love this album," said Mrs. Stewart. "That Elvis really knows how to sing, doesn't he?"

She started to dance to the music, singing along and moving around the living room with her cup in her hand. "I'm dreaming of a white Christmas," she warbled.

Mr. Stewart was putting a string of lights on the tree, wrapping it around the branches carefully. He went around and around, circling from top to bottom. Then he plugged the end of the lights in, and the whole thing sparkled all over with red, green, and blue twinkling flashes.

"It's so pretty!" cried Mrs. Stewart. "Now we can decorate it." She opened up a big cardboard box and lifted out a tray of brightly colored balls. Picking up a blue one, she handed it to Simon.

"You first, honey," she said. "I know how you like to hang the first ornament."

Simon took the ball and walked over to the tree. Reaching up, he hung it on a branch and stepped back.

"That's wonderful," said Mrs. Stewart. She took a red ball and hung it on another branch.

After the balls came a box filled with ornaments made out of hardened dough. They were shaped like snowmen and reindeer and candy canes, and they were painted bright colors.

"Remember when we made these?" Mrs. Stewart asked Simon. "It was in 1972, right after I discovered Foreverware. Which reminds me . . ."

She turned around and came walking toward the kitchen. I pulled the hallway door shut just before she saw me, and held it closed. I heard her go into the kitchen and come back again a minute later. I opened the door again and looked out. She was carrying a tray loaded with cookies and other treats.

"I've been saving these," she said, picking up a plate of gingerbread men and handing one to Simon. He took a bite and smiled.

"It's good," he said.

Mrs. Stewart smiled. "It should be. You and I made them together. Don't you remember? You rolled out the dough and helped cut them out. I even let you decorate them with icing."

Simon stopped chewing and looked at the gingerbread man in his hand. He'd bitten the head off, and he stared at the headless body, the chewed-up gingerbread still in his mouth. He closed his eyes and swallowed.

"How could I forget," he said.

Mrs. Stewart turned to hang another ornament on the tree. Simon stuffed the rest of the gingerbread man in between the couch cushions while her back was turned. Then he took a big drink of eggnog and wiped his mouth with his sleeve. For once, he'd found something that even he couldn't eat.

"Hey," said Mr. Stewart. "I hope you have some of your famous fruitcake."

"Of course I do," Mrs. Stewart said. "What would Christmas be without fruitcake?"

She went to the tray on the table and picked up a Foreverware container. She opened it and slid out a glistening fruitcake. The bits of candied fruit shimmered in the light of the Christmas tree as she cut a thick slice and handed it to Mr. Stewart. Then she cut another one and started to hand it to Rodney.

"No, thanks," he said. "I don't want any."

"What do you mean you don't want any?" Mrs. Stewart said. "Are you not feeling well? Maybe you should go upstairs and lie down."

"No, no," said Simon. "I feel fine."

I knew that the last thing he wanted to do was get into the Foreverware bed again. If staying out of it meant having to eat prehistoric fruitcake, he was going to do it.

"I'd love a piece," he said, taking the slice Mrs. Stewart offered him.

She watched as he took a bite and ate it. "Is it good?" she asked.

"Wonderful," said Simon, eating another bite.

"Well, save some for tomorrow morning when we open presents," said Mrs. Stewart. "We wouldn't want it all gone now, would we?"

"We sure wouldn't," said Simon, looking sick.

"Hey," said Mr. Stewart, looking at his watch. "It's after eleven o'clock already. We'd better hurry. Someone I know has to be in bed soon if he wants to get his rest for the big day.''

This was what I'd been waiting for. Bert and Ernie told me that the Stewarts had to be in bed by midnight at the latest in order for the Foreverware to do its work keeping them ageless. Their idea was to surprise them before they had a chance to lock Simon in his bed and get into theirs. According to the plan, things would be getting underway very soon.

Mr. Stewart went and got a book from the bookshelf and sat down on the couch next to Simon.

"Ready for the story?" he asked.

"What story?" asked Simon.

Mr. Stewart rubbed Simon's head. "Silly, you know what story. *The Night Before Christmas*. We read it every year. Then it's time for you to go to bed so You-Know-Who can bring you your presents. That is, if you've been good.''

"Of course he's been good," said Mrs. Stewart, sitting on the other side of Simon. "My little boy is always good.''

Mr. Stewart opened the book and began to read. " 'T'was the night before Christmas,' '' he said in a dramatic voice. "I just love this story.''

I was getting nervous. It was after eleven. Bert and Ernie should have been there, but there was no sign of them. Something must have happened. I listened to Mr.

Stewart reading the familiar story and tried to think of what to do.

" 'The children were nestled all snug in their beds,' " he read. "I wonder if they were Foreverware beds?" he added, and Mrs. Stewart laughed.

The story went on and on as I wondered what had happened to Bert and Ernie. Without their help, I didn't think I'd be able to get Simon out. If I tried and got caught, it was back to the basement for the rest of my life.

Mr. Stewart was getting to the good part now. " 'When up on the roof there arose such a clatter,' " he said.

All of a sudden, there was a loud thumping sound from upstairs, as though something heavy had fallen on the roof.

13

"What was that?" asked Mrs. Stewart.

"I don't know," said Mr. Stewart.

There was another series of thumps, as though someone were walking around over our heads. This was followed by a scraping sound. A few seconds later, a big cloud of ashes blew out of the fireplace and filled the room.

"What's going on?" shouted Mrs. Stewart, coughing.

There was a long whooshing noise as something slid down the chimney and came to rest in the fireplace. I watched, wide-eyed, as a figure stood up and dusted itself off. I couldn't believe what I was seeing. It was Santa Claus.

"Ho, ho, ho," he said, wiping the soot from his red suit and combing out the tangles in his long white beard. "Merry Christmas everyone."

Mr. Stewart threw the book down and jumped up. "Who are you?" he demanded. "How did you get in here?"

Santa wagged his finger at Mr. Stewart. "Now, don't be a naughty boy," he said, "or it will be coal in your stocking for sure."

"Is this some kind of joke?" said Mrs. Stewart. "If it is, it isn't very funny."

"It's no joke," said Santa. He reached up and pulled off his beard, revealing the face behind it. I recognized Bert—or maybe it was Ernie—underneath the disguise.

"The game's over," he said.

Mrs. Stewart screamed. Then she picked up the fruitcake. "You're not ruining my Christmas!" she yelled, and threw the cake as hard as she could at Bert.

It hit him right in the belly, and he fell backward, the wind knocked out of him.

"Get him!" she said to Mr. Stewart, who ran over and started wrestling with Bert on the floor. I wondered where Ernie was.

Mrs. Stewart grabbed Simon and started to drag him out of the room. "Get upstairs!" she shrieked. "Get into your bed."

"Not this time!" I yelled, pushing open the closet door and running into the room. I stood in her way, blocking the door. I glanced at the clock on the fireplace mantel. It was ten minutes to twelve.

"You!" she hissed. "I thought I took care of you."

"Well, you thought wrong," I said, and charged at her.

She dodged me, running back toward the Christmas tree. She was still holding onto Simon's pajamas, dragging him along with her. She stood on one side of the tree, and I stood on the other in a face-off.

"Let him go," I said.

"Never," she answered. "This Christmas isn't going to be spoiled like all the rest."

Behind me, Bert was rolling around on the floor with Mr. Stewart. They were huffing and puffing as first one and then the other was on top. I knew I had to take care of Mrs. Stewart soon so I could help him. I crept slowly toward Mrs. Stewart. She backed away. I kept going. Then I dove at her.

At the last second, she dodged out of the way, and I fell on the floor with a thud. She ran into the middle of the room, where she stood triumphantly with her arms around Simon.

"You'll never stop Christmas," she said.

I looked up and saw that she was standing right underneath the glitter ball from the disco. It spun above her head, catching the different colored lights from the tree. Suddenly, I had an idea. Reaching underneath the tree, I picked up one of the presents that was sitting there.

"That's what you think," I said, taking aim and throwing the box as hard as I could at the glitter ball.

The present sailed through the air. Mrs. Stewart

watched in horror as it hit the glitter ball with a smack. The ball lurched and broke free from the hook holding it up. It came crashing down on Mrs. Stewart, knocking her right on the head. She fell to the floor as the ball rolled off into the corner.

"Hold her there," I shouted at Simon. "We've got to hold her until midnight!" She was thrashing around, kicking and screaming as she tried to get up. Simon barely managed to keep her there as I unwound a tinsel garland from the Christmas tree and ran over. I knelt on the floor and wrapped the tinsel garland around Mrs. Stewart's arms, pinning them to her sides. Then Simon and I rolled her along the floor, wrapping her up tightly until she looked like some kind of weird Christmas mummy.

"Let me go!" she shouted, trying to break free.

While we had been capturing Mrs. Stewart, Bert had managed to wrestle Mr. Stewart under control. He was sitting on him, chuckling to himself. Simon and I grabbed another tinsel garland and used it to tie up Mr. Stewart.

"Thanks," said Simon when the two of them had been subdued. "I was beginning to think I'd be stuck here forever."

"What?" I said. "You didn't think I'd leave you here to be tortured by fruitcake, did you?"

I turned to Bert. "I'm glad you showed up," I said. "I was beginning to worry."

"It took us longer than we thought to get ready," Bert said. "Santa suits are hard to come by this time of year."

"Where's Ernie?" I asked.

There was a knock on the front door, and Bert went to open it. Ernie walked in. He was dressed like an elf, with pointy shoes and a green hat.

"Hello," he said. "Merry Christmas."

"Where were you?" I asked.

"Why, up on the roof, of course," he said.

Simon and I looked at him, puzzled.

"Someone had to look after the reindeer."

I decided it was better not to ask any more questions about how they'd gotten there. "What do we do with them?" I said instead, nodding toward the Stewarts.

"Just wait a minute," said Ernie, pointing to the clock above the fireplace. It was one minute until midnight, the time when the Stewarts were supposed to be in their Foreverware beds. "Watch what happens."

When both of the clock's hands were on the twelve, it started to chime the hour. After the first chime, I noticed that the Stewarts' hair was turning gray. By the third chime, their skin had begun to wrinkle. At six, they both looked about fifteen years older. And by the final stroke, they had aged about thirty years.

"Look at me," wailed Mrs. Stewart. "I'm old." She started to cry.

"Well, I guess that's it," said Bert. "Now we can all settle down for a long winter's nap."

"Not yet," I said. "There's still something else we need to do."

We left Ernie in the living room to look after the Stewarts while Simon, Bert, and I went into the basement to rescue the frozen boys. We opened each of the containers and put the boys on the floor to thaw. After about ten minutes, they started to open their eyes.

"Where am I?" said the first boy. His name was Thomas, and the label on his container said that he had been frozen in the Stewarts' basement since 1978. "How did I get here?"

As best as I could, I told them the story of what had just happened. It turned out that all of them had similar experiences to the one Simon and I had.

"I've been here since 1993?" said a boy named Joe. "My mother is going to kill me for being late."

"What about me?" said Ben, who had been Forever-wared since 1980. "I should be thirty by now! And I haven't even gotten into high school."

"Is Ronald Reagan still president?" asked Steve.

He'd come to the Stewarts' house in 1985. When I told him no, he laughed. "Well, at least something good has happened since I went into the deep freeze."

"Are we going to stay this way forever?" asked Bob, who had been kidnapped in 1989. "I mean, I guess it would be nice not to ever have to pay taxes or have a real job, but I'd kind of like to be able to drive myself to the movies and stuff."

The boys all looked at Bert. "Well," he said. "The freezerware was an experimental line of Foreverware. My father was working on it when he disappeared from his workshop one day. We never heard from him again, and all of his notes are missing. Because the product was never fully tested, we discontinued the model. We don't really know how it works or what its long-term effects are."

"So we're going to be this age forever?" said Thomas. "I'm going to have to take gym class all over again every year?" He groaned.

"Not necessarily," Bert said. "Ernie and I have been working on a little project. It's a microwave oven that makes things age more quickly. We could always use some volunteers to test it out."

The boys decided to go home with Bert and Ernie until they could figure out what to do. We went back upstairs to the living room, where Ernie was guarding

the Stewarts. He was sitting on the couch eating a gingerbread man.

"You should try one of these," he said. "They're
delicious."

All the boys groaned. "I don't ever want to see another one of those as long as I live," said Joe.

There was a barking sound, and Spike appeared from
underneath the couch. Only it was Spike all grown up.
The black fur around his muzzle was now tinged with
white.

"Hey," said Simon. "He must have hidden under
there during all the commotion."

Spike sat down in front of Ernie, begging for a
cookie.

"He's so cute," said Ernie to Bert. "Can we keep
him?"

"Well," said Bert. "We have wanted a dog."

"What should we do with them?" I asked Bert, ges-
turing toward the Stewarts. They had stopped struggling,
and both of them were asleep, snoring. I guess all those
years of staying young had finally caught up with them.
Their dancing days were over.

"They'll be fine," he answered. "They can't cause
any more trouble now."

We left the Stewarts sleeping in the living room
and went outside. Simon and I said goodbye to Bert
and Ernie and the boys and went to get our bikes.

Then we rode home to my house. Everyone was asleep when we got there, so we went up to the Secret Spot and wrote down everything that had happened before we forgot the details. Then, exhausted, we went to bed. For the first time in two days, we slept peacefully.

EPILOGUE

*T*he next morning, when Simon and I went down to breakfast, no one suspected what we had just been through.

"How was the camping?" my father asked. "See anything weird?"

I looked at Simon. "No, nothing weirder than usual," I said.

"Well, you're just in time," my mother said. "I actually made pancakes today."

"I'm not that hungry," I said. "I'll just have toast. Thanks anyway."

"Me neither," said Simon.

"Suit yourselves," my mother said. "Oh, I almost forgot. An older woman stopped by this morning. She said you and Simon had done some work for her."

I stopped buttering my toast.

"She said she and her husband were moving away," my mother continued. "Something about going to live with her son. Or maybe it was look for her son. I don't remember. Anyway, she left this for you. She said it was a thank you for all of your hard work."

My mother dropped a package on the table in front of me. It was wrapped in Christmas paper and topped with a red bow. I picked it up and peeled the paper away. Inside was a fruitcake and a card.

I opened the card, and something fell out. It was the picture Mrs. Stewart had taken of Simon during the birthday party. Then I opened the card. "Dear Marshall and Simon," it said. "Happy Holidays."

*T*he two of us were in the Secret Spot. Okay, so it's just my attic, but that's where Simon and I go to discuss all the evidence we've collected about Eerie. Also, sometimes we just hang out there. That day we were working on a jigsaw puzzle. It was a picture of a store called World of Stuff. The cool thing about World of Stuff is that you can get anything you want there. It's the ultimate in one-stop shopping. Mr. Radford, the owner, makes sure that the store is always stocked with pretty much everything from ice cream to comic books.

The jigsaw puzzle was Mr. Radford's latest promotional idea. Grinning wildly, he'd given me one as a free sample. "It'll sell like hotcakes," he'd claimed. "Not that our hotcakes sell all that well," he admitted. "Well, it'll sell *better* than hotcakes!"

The picture on the puzzle showed stacked shelves, the booths where Simon and I sat to eat our ice cream sundaes, and some racks of clothes. Mr. Radford was standing behind the counter, beaming, and his face took up about a third of the puzzle. It looked weird divided by the zig-zagging lines that separated the pieces, but that's not what was bothering me. It was an easy puzzle. But it wasn't until Simon held the last two pieces in his hand and I saw the spaces where I'd fit them in that it finally hit me. This was no ordinary puzzle. *This kind of thing isn't supposed to happen here,* I thought. *Not in Eerie.*

I held out my hand. "Hand them over," I said.

"Okay." Simon dropped the pieces into my palm.

I eyed them in disbelief. "What's going on here?" I asked.

Simon's eyes widened. "Maybe one's from a different puzzle?" he suggested, peering over my shoulder.

But when I placed the pieces neatly into their spaces, completing the puzzle, his face paled.

"I don't believe it." I stared at the assembled jigsaw. "All of the pieces are there. I've actually *finished* the puzzle."

"An unprecedented event," Simon agreed.

Anywhere other than in Eerie, finishing a jigsaw would be no big deal. But in Eerie, nothing is that simple. Neither of us had *ever* finished a jigsaw puzzle within the town limits. There was always at least one, and sometimes two, pieces missing.

And now . . . this!

"Weird," I decided. "I think Lodgepoole must be slacking off on his job."

"You think so?" Simon glanced down at the puzzle again. His gaze wandered across the floor. Suddenly he gasped. "You're wearing matching socks!" he exclaimed.

I looked down and saw that he was right. I was wearing two dark-blue socks. I guess I should explain that matching socks, like completing a puzzle, is another event that just never happens in Eerie. "Maybe he's sick," I mused.

Lodgepoole was one of the strangest people I had ever met. And, for Eerie, that was saying a lot. He had once run the Eerie branch of the Bureau of Lost. The Bureau sends out Certified Misappropriation Engineers to remove certain items from everyday life. Such as puzzle pieces and matching socks. Most of the things people think are lost have actually just been confiscated by the Bureau.

Of course, there are branches of the Bureau of Lost in every town in the world, at least according to Lodgepoole. But the Eerie division is much more thorough than the others. And that's because Lodgepoole is a very thorough kind of guy.

Simon and I knew that Lodgepoole's office was somewhere in Eerie, somewhere below ground. We'd both been there, and seen the enormous rooms filled with missing items, all labeled LOST.

When we'd been there last, we'd also met Lodgepoole's assistant, Al. While Lodgepoole oversaw the entire division, it was Al's job to actually go out and retrieve the Lost items. But when the Head Office found out about some mistakes Lodgepoole had made, they demoted him and promoted Al. Now Al ran the Bureau, and Lodgepoole was forced to do the dirty work—acquiring people's stuff.

At least, that's what he was *supposed* to be doing.

But I had *finished* a puzzle! *And* I was wearing matching socks. I shook my head. It was hard to imagine that Lodgepoole could have overlooked even one puzzle. But a puzzle and a pair of socks? "Something's definitely wrong with Lodgepoole," I said.

Simon nodded gravely in agreement. "So what are we going to do?" he asked.

I headed for the door. "The only thing we can do," I said.

"Sundaes at World of Stuff?"

"Right. If we're going to get to the bottom of this, we're going to need brain food," I answered.

We each put on a pair of mirrored sunglasses and

hopped on our bikes. Then we pedaled through Eerie toward the store.

I braked outside World of Stuff and propped my bike against the front window. Simon pulled up behind me and hopped off his bike. As we opened the door to the store, a bell rang alerting Mr. Radford to our presence.

"Ah, boys!" he called out, his moustache bristling as he smiled. "Did you finish the puzzle?"

"Yeah," I said. "It's a cool picture, Mr. R. Could we have a couple of hot-fudge sundaes?"

"Coming right up." Mr. Radford bustled around behind the counter. "Yessiree, I think that jigsaw's going to be a hot item. I'm thinking of following it up with other scenic views of the town. The Town Hall. The police station. The dump. . . . Why, the possibilities are endless!"

"Right," I agreed, wondering what kind of person would want to buy a jigsaw puzzle of the Eerie dump.

Simon and I sat down at one of the booths and Mr. Radford brought us our sundaes. I plunged my spoon into the mound of ice cream and fudge, and I could feel my brain clicking into gear. "Maybe we should look for Lodgepoole," I suggested between mouthfuls.

"What if *he's* lost?" Simon argued.

"Then that will be another clue," I replied. "We both know what he looks like, and where he usually operates. Why don't we split up and scour the town?"

"Okay," Simon agreed. "Just as soon as we finish these." He swirled his spoon around in the bottom of the ice cream dish.

Ten minutes later, we checked that our walkie-talkies were working, and then sped off in opposite directions. Simon was checking the laundromat—one of the best places in town to lose things—and the bus depot. I was looking into the police station and the banks. Pens were *always* missing from there. But when there was no sign of any activity in either spot, I called Simon to report my failure.

"Nothing here, either," Simon's voice crackled back over the radio. "Lodgepoole really is missing."

"Well, let's not give up," I decided. "Why don't you check the lockers at school? I'll check the Chamber of Commerce." I signed off and rode across to the Chamber. Once there, I slipped my mirrored sunglasses into my pocket and walked through the door. There was a bulletin board inside, and Lodgepoole liked to confiscate a few notes each day. But today the board was neat and clean, and more crowded with messages than I'd ever seen it. *Seriously weird,* I realized. When I checked in with Simon, he reported that there was no sign of Lodgepoole at the school.

Something was *very* wrong.

2 WEIRD
EERIE
INDIANA
The Center of Weirdness for the entire planet
FOX KIDS network
© 1997 Fox Kids
EERIE INDIANA is the center of weirdness for the entire planet, the number one landing site for UFOs in the country... But for some strange reason, only 13-year-old Marshall Teller and his 10-year-old friend Simon Holmes notice it!
Watch the #1 hit television series every week!
© 1997 Hearst Entertainment Inc. ™The Hearst Corporation